GO FOR THE JUGGLER

MAGICAL MIDWAY PARANORMAL COZY SERIES, BOOK #4

LEANNE LEEDS

BADCHEN PUBLISHING

Go for the Juggler
Published by Badchen Publishing
14125 W State Highway 29
Suite B-203 119
Liberty Hill, TX 78642 USA

Copyright © 2018 by Leanne Leeds

For permissions contact: info@badchenpublishing.com

GO FOR THE JUGGLER

CHAPTER 1

"WELL, THEY CAME," I TOLD FIONA AS I WALKED out of my yurt. "Devana, Gunther, and Ms. Elkins. I didn't bind them to the Magical Midway at all. They just poofed over here with us."

"At least you know some of what those two women claim is the truth," Fiona said. "I wonder if Gunther knew he was tied to us? And how? *How* are they tied to us? And since when?"

I took a deep breath and filled my lungs with the hot, dehydrated air. It was the beginning of summer in central Texas, and I could smell the familiar aridness. After the cool forests of the northwest, the difference was striking.

It smelled like home, though. Dirty, dusty, thorny home.

"I don't know. Right now, I don't want to think about it. I need to decompress my brain for a day or two."

"Was your mom excited that you were coming?"

"Yep. Dad seems to have given up his prejudice against the circus, finally. Granted, it's probably because I'm running it, and it's not any fun keeping the war with Uncle Phil going. We're on land just to the west of the shelter." I gazed to the east and pointed to a large house on a gentle slope. "See that? That's where I grew up. The shelter building is just a little bit behind it."

"It's quaint," Fiona said. "We're really out in the middle of nowhere, though. I don't see anything else for miles."

"That's Texas, at least outside of the cities. I know our address is Mickwac but, honestly, I don't even think we're technically part of the town. It's just the nearest post office to us."

"Likely better, anyway, since we just dropped a circus in the middle of your province," Fiona said. "How do we avoid being seen when we do that, anyway? I've always wondered but never bothered to ask."

"It's just part of the magic. People would think they saw us drive up, even though they didn't."

It felt good to be back home. I hadn't been back to the house since this started. Not since the day I walked into the cat shelter and found Samson glowing like he was radioactive. It was appropriate in a lot of ways that I was made ringmaster of the family circus on Halloween.

Since every day now was *basically* Halloween.

"Charlotte," Mark said as he walked up, arm in arm with Serena. "I think I came through here once when I was human. It's a nice part of the state. I look forward to taking Serena out to dinner in Austin."

Serena smiled and nodded. "It reminds me of the plains in Africa a little bit. I feel very at home here."

"We're on the same latitude line as the plains of Africa, so there are some similarities. Some ranches in Texas have a lot of African animals, too."

"As pets?" Fiona asked.

"As game to be hunted," Mark told her with a frown. "They capture the animals and let them loose in confined areas, then they shoot them from hiding places. The hunters are cowards."

Okay, time to change the subject.

"Is this your first time in this area, Serena?" I asked.

"Yes. I don't tend to venture far into the humans' area. It is *their* territory and not our own. Mark, however, wishes to share with me some of his human memories, and so this time I will go. *This* time."

Mark smiled faintly.

Mark may technically be the leader of the lion pride now, but I got the distinct feeling that Serena had no small say in the running, and Serena's twin sister Selena probably had an opinion or two herself.

"My sister will take care of the two who work to redeem themselves," she added. "Clearly, it is not done yet. Why are you still here, ringmaster, and not at the house of your parents?"

"Oh, I don't know. I was just taking in the air, chatting with Fiona. There's no rush."

"I would disagree with you. I would suggest that you go over to the house quickly," Serena told me, sniffing the air. "I am catching the scent of a mother female, and the scent contains shades of impatience and annoyance at her cub."

There wasn't anything creepy about that at all.

"She's right, Charlotte, you should go," Fiona agreed. "I'm going to go find Gunther and get to work on some of the research for the Witches'

Council meeting. Ningul has some maintenance to do on the big top."

"Tell my impatient brother I'll come by later." Uncle Phil blazed by us. "I have a little bit of work to get finished before I can relax."

Before I could respond, my uncle was halfway down the main midway path.

"Going to tell your parents about you and Gunther?" Fiona asked. Mark and Serena turned to go.

"I haven't really had the time to talk to them about a lot of what's going on, so I'll catch them up on everything, and see if they have any ideas that we haven't thought of. Including that."

"Good luck with *that*," Fiona rolled her eyes.

I suspected luck would not have anything to do with the conversation I was about to have with my parents. If worse came to worst, I could always rubber band back to the Magical Midway from my kitchen. And then move the Magical Midway. To somewhere in Siberia.

Sighing, I made my way toward the house.

"Let me see if I've got this right," my mother said slowly. "You have a huntress witch and a norn and the son of the only other ringmaster living in *your tent?*"

"Well, yurt. And I made some changes to it, so it's at least as big as this house, if not bigger. But yes."

"What does your uncle have to say about all of this?" Dad asked me.

They had taken the whole story better than I thought they would, though I left out the part about Gunther and me dating. They were speaking so carefully, and so slowly, and so deliberately, I suspected no one was yelling at me yet because they were still getting over the shock.

"He's been helpful with some information, but this whole thing honestly seems like a great big puzzle that just came to the forefront when I showed up. Gunther and the Makepeace Circus seem to have some things they've been told that I didn't know, but it was just a story."

"That's more than a story," my father said.

"I haven't put it all together yet. I'm told things that Gunther was unaware of. I *think* Devana knows things she's not telling anybody, and the same thing with Ms. Elkins."

"And Devana is…"

"The huntress witch," I told my mom. "Ms. Elkins is the norn."

"Is that a Norn with a capital n or a norn with a lowercase n?"

"Is there a difference?"

"A rather large one," Mom said as she glanced at my father. "There are rumored to be three Norns that hold some sway over the past, present, and future of man. Obviously, these are mythical beings. You can find quite a bit of information about them in Norse mythology."

"But we don't know if they exist," Dad pointed out. "It's another one of those stories of superpowerful godlike beings that we just don't know the truth of in these modern times. Did they exist? Do they exist now? We don't know."

"Norns with a lowercase n are not very common, but we do know they exist. There have been historical records of more than three of them. They also originated from the same general area. They are magical practitioners, though of what specific kind we don't know. Norns' goals are supposedly related to fate and destiny, which is the preoccupation of the Norns with a capital N," Mom explained.

"The three Norns are said to be female and divine. Their myth is that they have more influence over the course of man's destiny than any other beings in the cosmos. Influence, mind you, but not control."

"Do *you* think that's true?" I asked Dad.

"Like many things in the paranormal world, Charlie, unless you see it for yourself there's no way to know with any certainty," he said.

"Well, I don't know if she's capitalized or lowercase. I just know that I've seen Ms. Elkins be able to pierce through magic as if spells don't affect her. I did a spirit walk to the Makepeace Circus, and the old woman looked right at me."

"Regardless of capitalization, Charlotte, both of the creatures you've allowed into your home serve an agenda that you may not be aware of. Powerful creatures, at that."

"I understand that, Mom. That's kind of why I did it. I don't know what I don't know, but I at least realize I don't know it. And I'd rather have them closer. I at least have some chance to figure out what's going on when they are readily available."

"I'm not sure that's comforting to me," Mom told me, crossing her arms. "The forces that have gathered around you are quite powerful, Charlotte. More powerful than you may realize."

"I thought I was the most powerful witch in the world? Okay, one of two, anyway."

"When destiny and fate awaken, all the power in the world can't stand against it, Charlie." Dad gazed out the window toward the animal shelter kennels. "Your elevation has somehow awakened fate, it seems. In the face of destiny, the most powerful of witches in history have had trouble swimming against the tide."

"You're starting to sound like a seer, Alan," Mom chided Dad and poked him in the shoulder. "That's not like you at all."

"The dogs are…anxious. I think it's making me a little anxious as well."

I felt a wave of calm roll out gently from my mother, but my father held his hand up and shook his head. "Please, Martha, not today. I appreciate it, but I'd like to stay connected to them and make sure this doesn't get any worse."

The wave gently receded.

"Well, I did just drop a circus next to the animal shelter," I told him. "I imagine they can smell some of the predator shifters, and it's probably making them a little nervous."

"Maybe that's it," Dad said, sounding unconvinced.

I took a deep breath as I readied myself to explain that Gunther and I were now together romantically. That discussion, which my parents would not be happy about because Gunther and I were from different circuses, would inevitably lead into the prophecy Gunther was told about us getting married. I wasn't looking forward to saying any of this to my parents.

My parents who, by the way, previously emphatically warned me not to get involved romantically with Gunther.

Just as I was about to speak, sharp barks came from the kennel area and then stopped. The color drained from my father's face, and he held up his hand to silence us.

We froze, listening.

Then a cacophony of angry barking rose all at once. There was desperation, anger, and frustration to the snarls and howls that I had never heard echo through the hallways of our shelter before.

Dad jumped up from the table, knocking his chair over, and raced out the door. My mother and I took one look at each other and chased out after him.

Wayland Black, a cyclops from the Makepeace Circus, had once called me a heat merchant. It was a carnie phrase that denoted someone who attracted trouble over and over and over again.

We hadn't even been here for two hours, and already something was desperately wrong. I could feel it.

I just didn't know what it would take for me to stop it from happening everywhere I go.

Tiffany Drake lay on the concrete floor at the back of the dog kennels. I didn't know the girl, had never seen her before, but her name echoed like a scream from my father's mind.

The pool of blood beneath her head was still wet, and her hands were still wrapped around the broom she apparently had used to defend herself.

Unsuccessfully.

"No," my father whispered, leaning down to feel for a pulse. It was a futile gesture. I could feel and sense nothing from the college-age girl still as death on the floor, her blonde hair wet with red on the right side of her face.

"Who would do such a thing?" my father whispered.

"Dad, who is she?"

"A troubled girl," my mother answered. "She was arrested at her sorority for animal cruelty.

They played a prank against another sorority, kidnapped the sorority house's dog and displayed him in…Oh, the particulars are not important. The poor dog suffered and died from their *joke*," my mother said bitterly.

"She was serving her community service here," Dad said. "The judge hoped working here with the animals would help her to understand the magnitude of what she did."

"Alan, she's a human," my mother said to my father. "We're going to have to call the local police."

My father glanced at me with concern.

"They can't, Alan," Mom told him. "We had a delivery this morning, and the driver commented on the circus being there. In the past couple of hours, multiple people have driven by. The Magical Midway has already been noticed. If it disappears in three hours, it will just cause more suspicion. Even *we* can't explain that."

"Look, don't worry about us, let's worry about this poor dead girl," I told my mother. "We are the least of your worries. I'm sure I can handle it."

"I wish that were true, Charlotte," Dad said. "At least we own the land that you're sitting on in the human world, and we won't have to explain that. But there's no way to get around the fact that you, and your people, will be questioned about this."

"Don't you think we should worry about the dead girl before worrying about the circus?"

"The girl tortured a dog to death, Charlotte," my mother told me pointedly. "I feel bad for anyone that unnecessarily loses their life, but this girl was *relentlessly* narcissistic. She'd been here a week, and even with my powers, I couldn't engender any empathy in her that would stick. There is nothing we can do for her now."

"We're not trying to be unsympathetic, Charlie," Dad agreed. "But the girl was quite a spoiled twit, and a cruel one at that."

"I wouldn't lead with those observations when you talk to the police."

"No, probably not. I would suggest that you go back to the Magical Midway and alert your people as to what's going on. Your Uncle has dealt with inquiries from the humans before, so find him as soon as you can. I'll go back to the house and call the police."

My mother and I turned to walk out. After a few steps, we realized that my father was not following us.

"Alan?"

"The dogs," he said quietly, staring down at Tiffany's body. "They were angry, frustrated that they couldn't defend her. Even though she treated them with nothing but disdain the entire week that she was here…if they could've got out of the kennels, they would've given their lives for hers. They *would* have saved her."

My mother walked over to my father and put her arms around him. After a few moments, she gently steered him away from the body, and we all left the kennel.

Uncle Phil, we have a problem, I called out mentally as I stepped back onto the fairgrounds. *A volunteer at my family shelter was just murdered. My dad wanted me to grab you because he said you've dealt with this before.*

Does he want me to hide the body?

Are you kidding me? No! My parents will have to call the local police and they're likely going to investigate. Dad said you had experience with this.

It would be far easier just to hide the body, Uncle Phil grumbled. I spotted him at the other end of the clearing and made my way to join him. *Well, here's something I hoped I would never have to teach you. Samson, are you listening?*

I am, Samson said. I could feel the frustration and resentment bouncing through the air into my head from my guardian. *I had hoped to never have to do this again.*

"Do what?" I asked, walking into my expansive yurt with Uncle Phil. Looking around, I didn't see Samson in the common room.

I'm in your bedroom. Which is the only place I get any privacy anymore, now that you invited your stupid boyfriend and his foolish kitten to live here, Samson said.

Uncle Phil and I entered my semi-separate living area at the far side of the common room. At least my bedroom now had a door.

How long am I going to have to do this? Samson asked Uncle Phil.

"There is no way to know, Samson. I would think possibly a week, maybe even more. I don't know anything about the police here, or how long an investigation would be likely to take," Uncle Phil responded.

"What does he have to do?" I asked, confused.

"Samson is going to have to implement an illusion designed to fool the humans," Uncle Phil explained.

"Isn't that what we do more or less all the time, though?"

"Not precisely. For example, the centaur village has never been seen by a human. It's never been seen by a human wandering around the circus, because the magic *persuades* humans not to go there. During an investigation, it's highly unlikely that the magic will not arouse suspicion."

Police officers and detectives are much more methodical when looking for clues, Samson explained. *If "search the blue tent" is on a list they have of things to accomplish, that no one searches the blue tent will eventually arouse suspicion.*

"Detectives also tend to have a heightened intuition. On a daily basis, they look for clues and subtleties that normal people might dismiss," Uncle Phil added. "Our risk of discovery is much higher if we are the subject of an investigation. So, we have a mode that we can go into that will present a tangible, touchable truth to the detectives without arousing any suspicion."

However, I must maintain that illusion. It takes an incredible amount of energy, and I'll glow with it. Literally. That means I must stay out of sight the entire time.

"Why can't we just change everything for the duration of the stay here?"

"We don't have enough room to house everyone. Behind the illusion in a place that humans will be unable to enter, the living spaces and support for the paranormals will continue to be maintained. The police will simply have no access to it. Likewise, most paranormals will be unable to come out."

"Okay, so how do we do this? The police are going to be here any minute."

"First, you'll need to broadcast to everyone at the Magical Midway. I hate using the broadcast system because of how impersonal it is, but in this case, the situation calls for it."

Then, you let me know that you want me to put the illusion in place, Samson says. *In this case, Charlotte, the magic is not yours. The magic is mine.*

"What else can you do that I don't know about?"

Is this really the conversation you want to have right now?

"No, no, you're right," I said. "Okay, let's tell everyone what's going on, and then get this done. I want to get back up to the house, so I'm there when the police arrived."

"Good idea," Uncle Phil said.

I projected my voice into the ear of everyone at the Magical Midway. I wished after the announcement I had brought my mother down here to project calm because when I was done, it sounded like a thundering herd of cattle as everyone raced to hide.

"Okay, let's do it."

Samson glowed.

CHAPTER 2

DESPITE HAVING EXPANDED MY YURT, DEVANA AND Ethel Elkins rarely came to the common area. Both had been locked in Ms. Elkins' room for the past few days. Since I hadn't formally bound them to the midway, I was concerned about whether they had heard the announcement and understood what was going on.

I knocked on Ethel's door.

"We heard you!" the old woman screeched, and I winced. "Go away! The huntress witch and I are busy!"

"I just wanted to make sure that you knew about the police, and what was going on," I told her. "Glad you heard me."

"I hear everything!" the old woman snapped.

"Charlotte, we're just fine, and we are aware of the situation," Devana told me without opening the door. "We both appreciate you coming to check on us, but we're fine. We'll stay in Ms. Elkins' room until you let us know the situation in the human world has been dealt with."

"Okay, thanks, Devana," I called.

Silence.

"I feel like I should know what's going on inside there," I said to no one in particular.

"I'm sure you'll find out just as soon as they decide that you should know. Likely, they'll tell you at the most inconvenient moment." Gunther stepped out of his bedroom. "I doubt those two could do anything else, really."

"Aren't you worried that they've been locked in there for over a day now?"

"Honestly, I'm more worried about the police investigation," Gunther said, frowning. "Even I'm kind of suspicious that we showed up, and less than two hours later someone's dead a hundred feet from our fairgrounds."

"From *our* fairgrounds?" Gunther seemed to feel terribly possessive over *my* Magical Midway. We weren't even officially together a week yet.

"Oh come on, Charlotte, you know what I

mean." Gunther poured himself some tea. "I just got you to admit that you like me as more than a friend. We just decided to give a relationship a try. I'm not pushing my luck. It took me long enough to get you to this point."

"Har har har."

"You laugh, but I'm not kidding." Gunther brought me a cup of tea. "Anyway, here, some of that tea you like. I thought you'd be back over at your parents' house by now?"

"I was just about to head over there," I told him. I sipped from the steaming cup. "I want to see if I can figure out how the police are looking at this, and whether I need to be concerned that they're going to look at us. I have to admit, I'm a little freaked out, too, that someone got killed before the sun even set on our arrival."

"She's not a paranormal, though, right?"

"No, she was doing volunteer work here. She committed a human crime against an animal, and the judge sentenced her to do community service work here," I told Gunther. "That sometimes happens in our world."

"In the paranormal world or the human world?"

"Sorry, the human world."

"You still think of it as your world?" Gunther asked.

"Yeah, I guess I do. I spent almost thirty years of my life living in it. I guess I still think like a human first in a lot of ways."

"While you're up at the main house, I'm going to head back over to Ningul's. Fiona and I have been making some progress on understanding some of the things we can affect at the Witches' Council meeting."

"Why not just work here?"

"We, um…we wanted to make sure we had some privacy." Gunther's eyes darted over to Ethel Elkins' door.

"The older one or the younger one?" I asked as I got up.

"Yes," Gunther answered with a smile. He walked over and embraced me, carefully kissing my cheek. "We'll stay out of your way. We have plenty to do to keep us busy, and Fiona and I both figured you would want to spend time with your family."

"Yeah, just won't be in the way I hoped," I told him, kissing him back. "I'll try to be back for dinner."

"Remember the sundown rule," Gunther called after me.

For some reason, planetary energy played some kind of role in my tie to the Magical Midway. If I left the fairgrounds once the sun came out, I had to be back on the fairgrounds by the time the sun would set or I couldn't return until the following day. Although I'd followed it in the months since I'd come to the Magical Midway, I never really understood why.

At some point, hopefully, I would have spare time to examine the reasoning behind some of these rules.

Today, however, wasn't that day.

The house was bustling with activity.

My parents sat on the couch in the living room while a tall man about my age sat on a chair to the right. I could see his badge as his hand moved across his notepad. His hair was dark, as were his eyes, and there was something vaguely familiar about him.

"Charlotte," the man said politely, looking up. "It's been a long time. I haven't seen you since high school."

Squinting, I tried to place his face, but I just couldn't recall anyone as cute as this guy knowing who I was in high school. I didn't exactly have a peer group back then, and I suspected most of the other students graduated having no clue who I was. The man was built like a football player, meaty and thick and muscular and handsome.

I was *really* sure the football players didn't know who I was.

"I'm sorry, I'm not sure that I remember your name," I told him as I stepped toward the couch. "I was kind of shy in high school, though, so I'm surprised anyone that went to Liberty High remembers me."

"I remember you quite well, actually," he said standing up to extend his hand. "You sat in front of me in Ms. Green's world history class. I spent my junior year staring at the back of your head."

"Sorry about that," I said as we shook. "I hope my changing hairstyles kept you entertained, at least. I think that was my multicolored year."

"Detective Kyle Roberts."

"Detective, nice to meet you again," I said as he towered over me. "I think I'm starting to remember you now. You were on the football team, weren't you?"

"I was. I even got to play some football in college until my knee blew out." Detective

Roberts gestured down and shrugged. "Since fame, fortune, and fast cars were no longer in my future, I decided to come back to Mickwac and put my college degree to use."

"What did you major in?"

"Criminology."

"That sounds…creepy," I told him.

"It can be at times." He smiled and then turned back to my parents. "Unfortunately, there is a need for someone to understand why people do bad things."

"Charlotte, Detective Roberts was just asking about the circus," my father told me nonchalantly. "We didn't have too much information about it beyond the basics, so maybe you can help answer some of his questions."

"Sure, no problem." I sat down next to my father. "What kind of questions do you have?"

"When did you arrive and set up?" Detective Roberts asked as he sat back down in the chair.

"This morning, actually," I told him, breathing deep. I felt my mother waterfall calmness over me, as if I were standing beneath a magical Niagara Falls. "I hadn't been home in a while, and we didn't have any other dates we needed to make, so I thought we'd head here for a bit to visit my parents. It's been busy since I took over from my uncle."

"You brought your entire circus *just* to visit your parents?" Kyle Roberts asked evenly. "That seems like a costly side trip. Where were you before this?"

"At Big Bear Mesa," I told him.

"Big Bear? As in California?"

"I think so," I told him and cursed to myself as soon as the words left my lips.

"You *think* so?"

Since I didn't have many friends, and the few friends I had exploded in anger and recriminations right before I took over the circus, I had absolutely no practice answering personal questions posed by a human about my paranormal life. With no preparation or skill with deception, I hadn't realized how difficult it would be to answer the simplest of questions.

I had spoken with the humans on our midway multiple times and never had a problem, so I assumed I would be fine. But someone who knew me? Someone who wanted me to account for my whereabouts? This was far harder than I expected it to be.

"It was California. I'm sorry, we're a traveling circus. Because we travel so much, it's sometimes tough to keep track of what town or even what state you're in. We're just on the move all the time," I explained.

The detective stared at me for a few moments and then nodded.

I wondered if Kyle Roberts was satisfied with my answer, or if he just wanted me to *think* he was satisfied with my answer. My mother was throwing so many buckets of calm over me I could barely wiggle my own power through it to take the measure of the detective.

"And where are you going to after this?"

"Louisiana," I answered quickly. It was the only thing I could think of that could explain why going from California to Texas to visit my parents made sense.

"And you stopped here why?"

Didn't I just tell him that?

"To see my parents, but also to be able to do some maintenance on the rides and joints. We keep some of our larger machinery here to save on gas as we travel around," I told him calmly, clearly getting the hang of this lying thing on the fly.

I made a mental note to create a machinery storage building on the edge of the Magical Midway the moment I was back.

"Did you know the deceased?"

"No, I didn't," I told him.

"You didn't meet her this morning when you arrived?"

"No. The first time I saw her was when our family ran to the kennels because the dogs were going crazy," I responded. "That's when we found her on the floor."

"Do you have any problem with us questioning your employees, Charlotte?" the detective asked.

"I don't think so," I told him.

"You don't *think* so?"

"That's what I said."

"What would cause you to think that you might have a problem with me questioning your employees?" he asked me. His tone was growing slightly less friendly as he shifted forward.

"Carnies tend to have a lot of mistrust for the police," I told him, leaning forward as well. "I absolutely want to help you in any way that I can, and I'm sure that my folks feel the same. Circuses have just had a long history of local police wariness, and I don't want to cause my folks any more discomfort than I have to."

"Have you ever thought that maybe your

people mistrust the police because they've done bad things and they don't want to get caught?"

"No," I told him flatly. We stared each other in the eyes.

Detective Kyle Roberts watched me a few moments longer, and then nodded again to himself like he was engaged in a conversation I wasn't privy to. "I'm going to head out to the kennels so that we can take Miss Drake's body back to the morgue. Mr. Astley, we are sure all the dogs are secure?"

"Yes, Detective, absolutely sure. I can't promise that they'll be quiet, but I can promise they won't get out."

"Thank you, sir," he nodded and walked toward the back door. "Oh, and one more thing. Charlotte?"

"Yes?"

"Don't leave town, okay? Not just you. Let's make sure the circus hangs around until we fully understand what happened here. That shouldn't be a problem for you since you were coming for a visit. Okay?"

I nodded as the rest of the police officers followed Detective Roberts out the door.

"Well, I guess that answers the question as to

whether our being here is causing any suspicion," I told my parents.

"Maybe we *should* have had Charlotte leave," my mom told my dad.

"Too late now," he said. "But so far, all the police have done is ask questions. That's what they're supposed to do. There is no indication that they have any particular suspicion about the circus."

"They are police, Dad. Police are always suspicious of carnies."

"Did you get any sense of what he was thinking, Charlotte?"

"No. Mom was throwing so much of her power at me to keep me calm that I couldn't really use my own talent," I told him.

"For now, let's just be a little cautious, but I don't think there's any reason for concern just yet," Dad said. "I understand the girl has quite a colorful history. No doubt Detective Roberts will be looking into that first."

"I was a little shocked to see him," I told Gunther back at Ningul's. "Actually, I wasn't shocked to see him, because I didn't recognize him. I *was*

pretty surprised that he recognized me right away."

"Well, this is the Astley Animal Shelter," Gunther pointed out as he shuffled papers on Ningul's dining room table. "Since he is a detective, he probably knew about the place and your association with it before he even showed up."

"Remember, Charlotte, before your father and uncle entered into this ridiculous rivalry, the circus used to winter here on this land," Fiona reminded me. "All that was many years ago before my time, but the humans tend to like recording their history. The circus stopping back by shouldn't be that odd an occurrence."

"You have a problem," Uncle Phil announced, stomping into Ningul's cabin uninvited.

"I always have a problem," I told Uncle Phil and shrugged. "Is this a new problem or a problem I already know I have?"

"I don't know if you're aware of this problem, Charlotte. Considering how little you check with me, I'm continually surprised that I know anything at all happening on the Magical Midway anymore."

"Geesh, what's gotten into you?"

Uncle Phil sighed and sat down at the big,

wooden dining table. Swallowing, he rubbed his scraggly face with his hands and shook his head back and forth as if to clear it.

"I apologize," my uncle said when he looked up. "That actually was very uncalled for. I don't like dealing with the human world, or the human law enforcement people. It puts me out of sorts."

"It's okay, Uncle Phil, I get it." I placed my hand on his shoulder and squeezed. "I got questioned by a detective when I went up to the house, and even with my mother helping to keep me calm, I was pretty nervous myself."

"Anyway, to the problems," Uncle Phil said, patting my hand. "Between the huntress witch taking up residence in our circus, the murder that took place at the Astley Animal Shelter, and the shift into protection mode, the residents here are quite concerned."

"Maybe that's a good thing, Uncle Phil. Until the police get done with their investigation, we do have some risk of exposure. Maybe it's better that people are more nervous than comfortable. You know what I mean?"

"Yes, well, as long as they don't panic, Charlotte, that may be true. If they panic, it could put us at greater risk than if they are calm, especially with the police poking around."

"If they get really scared, most of the shifters will shift," Fiona pointed out. "If that happens, there won't be enough human looking people left at the circus for the police to make sense of this place. It will look like our people ran and scattered to the wind. That could make them look closer at us, which we don't want."

"Let's have a meeting in the big top," I told the group.

"In the visible big top or the invisible big top?"

"I...the *what* now?

"Charlotte, Samson is ensuring that every single building in this place has a false front, essentially. Humans cannot go beyond that false front. Paranormals can, and it's where most are currently hiding. Didn't you notice when you came back over here that the circus essentially looked like a ghost town?"

"How does that keep suspicion down with the police, Uncle Phil?"

"Well, it is Texas, and it's hot. I imagine if the police glanced over here, they would assume that everyone is inside or they left to go visit their own family."

"My head hurts," I told him.

"Snap out of it, ringmaster," he responded looking up at me. "This is likely the most risk that you've faced since being elevated to your position. I would highly suggest that you take it seriously."

"Out of everything going on, everything that the Witches' Council is pulling, you think *this* is the most risk that we've faced?"

"Charlotte, the rule to not expose us to the human world is an old one, and a strong one. That is not some Witches' Council dictate. That is a separation of realities woven into the very fabric of our world. The humans cannot know for certain we exist."

"Why?" I asked him.

He stared at me, and blinked. Gunther and Fiona looked at each other uncomfortably.

"What do you mean, why?"

"I mean just what I said. Why? I know about the rule. I know that the rule is a big deal. I know humans being exposed to the fact that we exist is supposed to be dangerous. I'm just curious as to why."

"Why? You want to know *why*?" Uncle Phil asked, getting even more agitated.

"Yes! It's a simple question. Why is it so serious?"

"The humans would move against us, Charlotte," Fiona said. "They moved against us before. It's why we had to withdraw from the world and live in the shadows."

"They don't hunt down psychics in the streets anymore," I pointed out. "Or drown women to find out if they're witches."

"It wasn't as long ago as you might think that they *did*," Uncle Phil argued back. "Once they found out our power and our riches, they would hunt us down like dogs in the street."

"First, no one hunts down dogs in the street. Second, we don't think very well of humanity, do we?"

"We have reason not to think well of humanity, Charlotte," Gunther pointed out. "We don't have a very good history with humans."

"I know that you're fond of having these philosophical discussions, but do you think we could perhaps have them at another time when we were not under a cloud of human and paranormal suspicion?" Uncle Phil asked with exasperation.

"Sorry! It was just a question."

"Question our reality at another time," Uncle Phil said. "There's one more thing."

"What is it?"

"The dead girl's ghost is in the haunted house, and she is not very happy about it."

CHAPTER 3

"Do you think he does that on purpose?" I asked Gunther as we hurried toward the haunted house.

"Does what?"

"Bury the lead. Wait to tell me the *most* important, most pressing piece of information until the very last part of the conversation."

"I doubt that he thought Tiffany Drake's ghost appearing in the haunted house was very important," Gunther said as we walked. "After all, she's dead, and we're not here to solve a crime. We are here to make sure that we don't get accused of a crime. Well, now, anyway."

"Look, this is the world I grew up in. I realize in the paranormal world investigation is kind of whacked out, but the human world is pretty methodical about everything. You know what the easiest way is to stop the police from investigating?"

"What?"

"To have the murder case *solved*. That would make them go away. We have resources that they don't have, so we may as well see what we can find out." I climbed the steps to the haunted house door. "At least it's cool inside there. If the ghosts all gather around us, it will be positively balmy. We may even need a jacket."

We slipped inside the always-dark haunted house, and the quiet of the place wrapped around me. There was something about the Gothic decor and the Victorian era furnishings that made me feel at peace when I came in here. It seemed weird in a way because this was a totally legit haunted house. It was designed to be creepy, the place we sent the humans to be scared out of their wits.

For me, though, it felt like a church. Quiet, peaceful, dark and serene.

"You came for the new ghost!" little Anna squealed as she popped into visibility in front of me. Gunther jumped and slammed against the wall in surprise.

"Gunther, this is Anna. Anna, this is my boyfriend, Gunther," I introduced them. "Anna was one of the first ghosts that I met when I came to the Magical Midway."

"How do you do, Anna?" Gunther said with a small bow.

"How do I do *what*?" Anna asked him, tilting her head in confusion.

"It's just a way of saying that it's nice to meet you," Gunther responded with a chuckle.

"Oh! Good. It's nice to meet you, too, even though I've heard you talk, and I've heard you talking and talking about Charlotte, and I know you like her a whole lot," Anna said, pointing her little hands at his chest. "She likes you a lot, too. Are you going to have babies? I think it would be cool to have babies. No one's had babies in a while."

Gunther smiled widely.

"Anna, where is your mom?" I asked quickly, cutting the little girl off before that conversation went further.

Thank goodness it was dark in here, and no one could see me blushing.

"Mama said she can't come down," Anna told me seriously. "She has to stay upstairs because of Gunther. But I'm supposed to tell you she has to stay upstairs because she doesn't feel well, and not tell you that it's because of Gunther," Anna finished. Then the little girl tilted her head and put her tiny hand over her mouth. "Oops. I didn't do that right, did I? Mama said I need to think before I speak more."

"You did fine, Anna. Tell your mom I hope she feels better."

I wondered why Gerda couldn't come down because Gunther was in the haunted house. Was there some problem between the matronly ghost and the Makepeace Circus? As I went over my previous interactions with Gerda, I suddenly realized how little the spirit had shared with me about her own history.

"I will. Are you here about Tiffany?"

"I am. You said you had a new ghost. Did she come here?"

Anna made a face as if she sucked on a lemon, and nodded.

"She's *mean*. She's mean to *everybody*. Sometimes when new ghosts show up I don't understand why they had to become ghosts when they became ghosts," the little girl said. "It's sad, you know? But Charlotte?"

"Yes?"

"I *totally* understand why someone would want *her* a ghost. I *sure* do."

"Has she said anything about who wanted to make her a ghost?"

"She's *mad* at them," Anna responded. "She's upset they made her face look funny. Like, really upset."

"Did she say *who* made her face look funny?"

"She didn't see them," she said while shaking her head no. "She was stuck for a while, and when she finally popped out, there wasn't anybody there anymore."

"Stuck?" Gunther asked.

"She probably wasn't killed instantly," I told him. "My guess is it took some time for her to pass away, and by the time she left her body the person that killed her was gone. It doesn't take that long to run out of the area where she was killed."

"She said she was very surprised," Anna told us. "She didn't see anyone come up to her. Well, no one was there besides the people that were looking to adopt the doggies."

"Did she say how many people were there in the kennel at the time?"

"She thought they had all left."

"Don't your parents require a sign-in to go back to the kennels?" Gunther asked.

"No, we never have," I told Gunther. "They can't take them out of the kennels without someone from the shelter unlocking the door, so there never seemed to be a reason for it. Once they decide they want to meet a dog, *then* we get their information. That way anyone can go back there and just look. We try to make it easy for folks."

"Can't your dad just ask the dogs?"

"I imagine he has," I told him. "When I left him this morning, I wasn't planning on looking into this, though, so I didn't ask. We probably should swing by there after this. I didn't get there early enough to hear what he told Kyle, so I'm not sure."

"Kyle?"

"The detective."

"You're on a first name basis with the detective?" Gunther raised his eyebrow.

"Would you quit? I went to high school with the guy."

"I saw the big detective, and he's a cutie patootie," Anna unhelpfully added. "He's big and handsome!"

"You know, for a little girl, you notice some *seriously* inappropriate things," I told her.

"After five hundred years, I know when someone is cute," she told me, crossing her arms. "Like him, he's cute." She pointed at Gunther.

"Thank you, Anna, I appreciate the compliment," he said and smiled at her. "I think, though, it would be really helpful if you took us to go meet Tiffany."

"Ugh. You *really* want to meet her? She's really *really* not nice," Anna warned us again. "If she didn't die and she became a grown-up? She would have been a *very* mean lady."

"Yep, I think we need to. Can we come in?"

Anna sighed. She nodded and moved toward the threshold that led to the interior part of the walkthrough haunted house. "Follow me. I know where she was last throwing a fit. She throws long fits, so I bet she's *still* there."

The haunted house was set up so that patrons entered in and were led through all the rooms of a rickety old Victorian-era mansion. Each chamber was elaborately decorated, and humans were funneled through the consecutive spaces by a maze-like path. Each area, of course, was manned by one or more ghosts that did their best to make visitors scream in fright.

When the ride was closed, the haunted house was merely the house where the ghosts lived. Aside from the Victorian furnishings, thick soundproofed walls, and darkness, it resembled a frat house. Well, if they had frat houses in the Victorian era.

"They did," Gunther said.

"They did what?"

"Have fraternities in the Victorian era. The first frat in the United States was founded in 1825. I read a human book on it once."

I stopped walking and turned to stare at Gunther in shock.

"What?" he asked, concerned.

"How did you know I was thinking about that?"

"What are you talking about? I heard you. You were talking about how this resembled a frat house."

"No, I *wasn't*," I insisted. "I was *thinking* about it, but I didn't say anything out loud."

"Of course you did! I *heard* you clear as a bell," Gunther said, stepping closer to me.

"Gunther, I *swear* to you, I didn't say *anything*

about it out loud. I'm not messing around with you. I was thinking it as we walked, but I never said any of what I was thinking out loud at all," I told him.

"I think you have new powers, too," Anna said.

"What do you mean, new powers?" Gunther asked the little girl.

"Well, we can pop all over the place and be invisible now," Anna said after she stopped and turned to face us. "One day all the ghosts just woke up, and we could do it again. Mama said we used to be able to do it, and then we couldn't do it anymore, and now we can do it again. So maybe you used to be able to read minds, and then you couldn't, and now you can!"

"I'm not sure it's related, but Anna has a point," Gunther said. "I did go from being a half-witch to a full witch. We were dealing with so much that I never really stopped and explored what that might mean. Maybe I *did* get new powers out of it."

"It seems really strange that it would just happen now," I pointed out. "Why couldn't you pick up on what I was thinking before this?"

"Honestly, Charlotte, this may very well be the quietest moment we've had since I transitioned," Gunther smiled. "Maybe I just needed to be somewhere calm and peaceful for it to bubble up and happen."

"You and I have had quiet moments together. I mean, we spent a lot of time in the yurt together just you and me."

"Yes, but I couldn't really say that I was *relaxed* during a lot of those moments."

I blushed.

Gunther tended to cover his nerves really well, then. It was sweet that he was nervous around me. Even so, I had a nagging feeling that his sudden ability to read my mind wasn't just a new power he picked up after he became a full witch.

"Well, maybe I'll be able to teach *you* a thing or two for a change," I told him. "In any case, we probably need to put this aside and deal with it later. Oh, and Gunther? Stay out of my head."

"Um. I'm not sure I know how to do that," Gunther admitted as we began walking again.

"Well, that's the first thing you're going to learn," I told him. "Fortuna should be able to help, too."

I added helping Gunther control his mind, so he didn't rummage willy-nilly through people's heads, to my long list of things I needed to do.

Tiffany Drake was more than mad.

Tiffany Drake was *enraged.*

The blonde girl was shrieking at the three ghosts that circled her. They pleaded with her to calm down so they could talk to her, but she simply screamed back at them.

"I'm nineteen years old! I'm not supposed to be dead! I'm certainly not supposed to be stuck in some old, dark, horribly dirty house with a bunch of nerdy ghosts that are pretending they walked out of history! I want to talk to my father!"

Pictures rattled on the wall, and a lamp crashed to the floor.

If the young woman's face could change color, it would likely be red. Walking into the room, I was grateful for the absence of her body. She rushed me so fast and screamed so loud that I likely would have been covered in spittle if she had a mouth.

"Get me out of here! These stupid idiots told me you were in charge! I don't know what you people have done to me, but I absolutely and completely *refuse to be dead*! I haven't even graduated from college yet! Take me to my father, and he can fix all of this!"

"Tiffany, my name is Charlotte Astley, and if you don't calm down *none* of us will be able to help you," I told her in as soothing a voice as I could muster while being shrieked at. "I am very sorry about the day that you had, but Gunther and I are here to try and help you."

"Help me with what? *I'm a bloody ghost!*"

"Well, you're *not* bloody," Anna matter-of-factly told her. "We can make ourselves look scary and bloodied, but we don't have any skin. Or blood. So no one is really a *bloody* ghost."

"Someone shut that stupid child up," Tiffany snapped.

"Hey now, let's dial it back a little, huh, sister?" I told the angry sorority girl a little more sternly. "There's no reason to be rude or mean to anyone in this room. We are not responsible for the fact that you're here, and we *are* trying to help you."

"How do *I* know that you're not responsible for me being dead? I don't know who killed me. It could have been *you*. It could have been any of you! *I want my father!*" Tiffany screeched again as she paced around the room, her translucent hands balled into fists.

I suspected that the shouting, mumbling, and pacing would continue unabated. The girl just did not want to accept what had happened to her, and she was unwilling to calm down to listen. A wall of denial was being thrown off in every direction.

"Can you send Samson to get your mother? Maybe she can calm a ghost down," Gunther said.

"No, we can't bother Samson while he's holding the illusion. Why don't you go and get my mother? I don't know if her power works on ghosts, but it seems to work on everything else, so it's worth a shot. We're not going to get anything out of Tiffany like this, and her current state isn't doing her any good, either."

"Charlotte?" I heard my mother call.

"We're back here, Mom," I called back.

As my mother stepped into the room, Tiffany whirled on her. Shaking a pointed finger, she screeched even louder. "This is all your fault! I told you that I didn't want to work in the back room! *I told you!* You made me do it and now *look what happened*! I'm dead and trapped in *some kind of circus hell-scape!*"

"You know, no one invited you here, young lady," one ghost snapped at her. "You made your way to our house all on your own."

"I know, right?" Anna agreed with her. The older and younger ghosts crossed their arms judgmentally at the newest member of their little house.

"Tiffany, I am so terribly sorry that this happened to you," my mother told the girl in a soothing voice I recognized from my teenage tantrum phase. "This is our family circus, and as a ghost, you would have likely chosen to come here on your own even if you're not fully aware of why."

"I would never come to this filthy place! I live in a mansion, summer in Paris, and spend my Saturdays at a country club! *I would most certainly never choose to come to a place like this!*" Tiffany's voice was still louder than would be appropriate for conversation, but I could see the rage slowly draining from her.

"Well, I never!" the older ghost standing next to Anna exclaimed. She and the other two ghosts that had been attempting to get through to Tiffany floated over to, and then through, the wall.

"Of course, my dear, but the rules of the living and the choices of the living are not always the same ones that apply once we pass on," Mom told her. She slowly approached the girl. "I imagine that you simply gravitated toward the nearest location that held others like you, so you wouldn't be alone. It is a primal spirit urge we have. To not to be alone."

"None of these people are like me," Tiffany scoffed, but in a much more normal volume. "I would never be around people like this."

"Of course, dear, but these are your people now, and they wish nothing more than to help you through this," Mom cooed and came to stand directly before the delicate girl.

"I want my father," Tiffany responded, staring into my mother's eyes.

"Unfortunately, my dear, it is unlikely that your father would be able to see you. While some humans can see ghosts quite clearly, the vast majority of human beings cannot."

"*You* can see me," she said.

"Yes, but I am *not* human," my mother responded and smiled. "All of us in this room are supernatural in nature. So are *you*, now. We are terribly sorry that you lost your human world before you were ready, but we wish to make your transition into our paranormal world as easy as possible for you. You are not alone, Tiffany. We *will* help you, I promise."

"But I don't *want* to be dead," the girl whispered.

"I am so sorry, dear," my mother whispered back. "What happened to you was tragic, and we are so sorry this is so difficult for you."

Tiffany's deflation was complete, and she moved to sit in a velvet chair in the corner of the room. "I don't know what I'm supposed to do. I mean, *what* am I supposed to *do*?"

"First, I think we need to know what you remember about your attack," I told her. "With so many paranormals here, I would really like to get us away from the human investigation as quickly as possible. It'll give us much more time to focus on helping you."

"Nothing, really," she said, screwing her face up as she concentrated. "I was sweeping the back storage room, the one behind the curtains?"

My mother nodded.

"There weren't very many people looking at the dogs, and I had checked to see whether any of them needed help, but they didn't."

"Did any of them act odd when you spoke to them? Ask you any weird questions, make you feel nervous for no reason?" I asked.

"No, not really," Tiffany said. "Nobody was

really very talkative. I just told them to let me know if they wanted to see any of the dogs, and I would get someone to unlock the kennel for them."

"After that, you went into the back room?" Gunther asked. Tiffany nodded.

"I talked to the nice couple, and then the guy, and then the other guy—"

"Wait, there was a third man?" I asked her with surprise.

"Yes, there was the couple and then one guy and then another guy," Tiffany responded. "The last guy had this huge hoodie on, though, and I couldn't see his face."

"Mom, I thought you said there were only three people out there? The couple and one other guy?"

"I don't remember seeing the fourth person, Charlotte. We do have cameras at the parking lot and around the property, though. If the police didn't take the entire recording system, we should be able to look at the recordings and see if there was someone else."

"Can I *please* see my father?" Tiffany asked. Though the girl's anger had dissipated, her fear was still present. I suspected that Mom was allowing her to feel some things so she could work through them. Numbing the girl would not serve her well.

Not to mention the fact that as soon as Mom left, she would probably turn back into a shrieking banshee.

"Again, you can probably go see your father, but it's unlikely that he would be able to see you. Has he ever told you that he has any kind of talent for seeing ghosts? Any weird stories from when he was a kid?"

"No," Tiffany told me. "I just want to see him when he comes here. Can I leave this house? I don't think he would come over to the circus. Can I go back over to the shelter?"

"Wait, why do you think your father would come here?"

"My father is Anthony Drake. There's no *way* that he wouldn't come here. He's going to be really angry, and he doesn't trust the cops."

My mother and I stared at each other in shock.

"Did you know?" Mom shook her head no.

"Who's Anthony Drake?" Gunther asked.

"My father," Tiffany said.

"A gangster," my mother said.

"Trouble," I told him.

CHAPTER 4

MOM LED TIFFANY BACK TO THE MAIN HOUSE
while Gunther and I headed toward my yurt to
check on Samson.

"I can't believe Mom agreed to this without
finding out who her father was," I complained as
we walked across the uncharacteristically quiet
Magical Midway.

"Why is that?" Gunther asked.

"Why is what?"

"Why can you not believe that your mom
agreed to this without finding out who her father
was? Is it common for offspring in the human
world to have dangerous criminal parents?"

"No," I admitted. "Actually, there's no real

reason she would've asked, I guess. I'm just aggravated. This complicates things."

"How so?"

"Anthony Drake *owns* Mickwac. I mean, like, not in a good way. He is such a creep. I went to school with his younger brother, and the guy was an *absolute* jerk. Rich, entitled, abusive. I found out later that they made their money through some fairly illegal dealings."

"Illegal how?"

"Allegedly? Insurance fraud. They pay people to take falls, to slip on floors, to drive in front of semi-trucks. He's a lawyer, and so he sues on their behalf, wins a mountain of cash through a trial or a settlement, pays the person that faked the accident a pittance and keeps the rest."

"That sounds so dishonest," Gunther said as we drew closer to my yurt.

"It's more than dishonest. It's illegal. And it's dangerous. A few years back some kid drove in front of a semi-truck to cause an accident. The driver was looking away at the time and didn't stop as fast as usual. The kid died."

"That's horrible," Gunther gasped.

"Yup, it is," I agreed. "Lots of horrible things happen in the world."

"In both worlds, apparently."

"Anyway, Anthony Drake is very protective of his little fraud scheme, so he lines the pockets of the local politicians, donates money to the police funds, slips cash into the open palms of law enforcement. It's all very corrupt, but he flat out owns this town. It's one of the reasons we put the shelter outside of the city limits. He's definitely in with the county, but not quite as deep."

Walking into the yurt, we saw Ms. Elkins' door was still closed. The cavernous house was quiet except for a muffled murmuring indicating that Devana and Ms. Elkins were still hard at work.

"What do you think they're doing in there?" I whispered to Gunther.

"I don't think you need to whisper," Gunther answered. "Ethel can hear what you say on the other side of the Magical Midway. Whispering won't keep her from hearing this conversation. As for what I think they're doing? I have no idea."

The quiet murmuring stopped.

"Just you get on with your business!" Ethel Elkins screeched from behind the door. "You don't worry about us!"

"See?"

"If we ever do take over the Witches' Council and we get the chance to push for new laws?

Right to privacy is going to be *high* up on my list
of things I want to deal with," I told Gunther and
slowly opened up the door to my bedroom.

Samson was lying in the center of my king-
sized bed, a black circle in the middle of the
spring-shaded comforter. He looked completely
normal...Completely normal, that is, if you could
ignore the bright white light emanating
from him.

"Samson? Gunther and I just wanted to check
on you and make sure you are doing okay," I said
quietly.

I'm fine.

"Is there anything you need? Anything we can
get you?"

No.

Ever since Samson had begun to maintain the
elaborate illusion designed to hold up even in the
face of a police investigation, he had become
uncharacteristically quiet. My uncle had warned
me not to bother him too much because of how
taxing this was on him, but I worried. I missed his
sarcastic banter, his wordy responses to the most
straightforward questions. Responses that only
sometimes contained an answer.

"Charlotte, he seems fine. I know you're
worried about him, but I'm sure he'd let you

know if there was a problem." Gunther gently placed his hand on my elbow to guide me away.

I would. Go.

I reluctantly made my way toward the door. I wasn't sure what else I could do.

Pausing, I looked back.

Despite the things I had learned about the paranormal world, about myself, about the Magical Midway, the mystery that eluded me the most was Samson. My lack of knowledge about my guardian frustrated me. I felt powerless to help, and I knew without a doubt this was a struggle for him. I could feel the strain in our bond.

Stop worrying. Go.

"I love you, Samson," I told him for the first time.

Me, too. Go.

The police had left the main house. I knew they were still taking pictures and walking around the back part of the property, but I had confidence in Samson's ability to protect the Magical Midway, so I didn't worry too much.

"Was Tiffany able to tell you anything more

about what happened to her?" I asked my mother as Gunther and I walked into the kitchen.

It was funny, really. The kitchen was my mother's sanctuary, the place where people sat to talk about serious issues. As people unburdened, Mom would hand them whatever drink or food she felt they needed. She was a kitchen witch through and through, and the kitchen table was the altar she presented to you so you could let your burdens down.

Even though Tiffany Drake could eat nothing anymore, she sat at the head of the kitchen table altar so Mom could help her unburden.

"No, Charlotte, she truly doesn't remember anything more that could help," Mom said, continuing to clean the dishes. "Your father is in the back office looking to see if the other man is on any of the security tapes. She has a bit of a description, but it's very generic."

"You know, I'm sitting right here and can hear *everything* you're saying. Anyway, I didn't know I would *have* to remember him," Tiffany snapped through my mother's continued downpour of enforced calm. "When I woke up this morning, I was unaware someone was going to bash my skull in, and I certainly didn't know it would be someone at the shelter."

"Speaking of that, I have a question," I said sitting down next to Tiffany. It was hard to speak to the ghost in a bright room. The sparkling transparency of Tiffany's apparition almost disappeared beneath the rays of streaming sunlight. I started to sincerely appreciate the darkness of the haunted house.

At least I could see who I was speaking to.

"Ask away," she answered.

"Why did you have to serve community service for what you did? Considering who your father is, frankly, I'm surprised you got any punishment at all," I told her.

"Right, because I'm Anthony Drake's daughter I would no doubt get out of any kind of punishment, right? Because my father's never prosecuted for anything that people think he does, we're all corrupt and the law can't touch us, right?"

"I don't know that I would've put it like *that*, but essentially, yes. That's my question."

Tiffany glared at me angrily, and then suddenly shrugged.

"I guess it doesn't matter what I say now. I wasn't *supposed* to be punished," she snapped at me, fuming anew. "Daddy *promised* me that his lawyer would show up at the hearing and make sure the proper people were told how it was going to go. His assistant set the whole thing up, he said."

"I thought your father was a lawyer?" Gunther asked.

"He is, but he *has* a lawyer, of course. There are different types of lawyers, you know."

"You mean corrupt and not corrupt?"

Tiffany narrowed her sparkling, translucent eyes at him.

"I think she's talking about the fact that her father is an ambulance chaser, and she needed a criminal defense attorney. They are not the same in the human world," I told Gunther.

"That's *offensive*," Tiffany said. "True, but offensive. She's right. Daddy sent his criminal attorney to defend me and get me out of everything. Only he didn't show up. I was just there all by myself, and I didn't know what to do. Some public defense attorney came up to represent me, and before I could blink, I pled guilty and agreed to all this stuff. Even Daddy couldn't undo it once he found out, it all happened so fast."

"Who is the public defense attorney that came up to represent you?"

"I don't know," Tiffany responded. "He told

me he was my Daddy's attorney, but he wasn't. He couldn't have been. If he were, this wouldn't have happened."

"Wait a minute, back up a second. Did you know that the public defense attorney wasn't your father's attorney at the time you pled guilty?"

"No. He just apologized for being late, so I assumed it was Daddy's attorney. I never met his attorney before. Why would I?"

"So why do you now think he was a public defender?"

"I don't know," Tiffany shrugged. "Afterward when Daddy found out what happened, he was super mad and said it couldn't have been his attorney. Michael said it was probably just some attorney that was assigned because I didn't have one. Because I was indignant."

"Indigent?" I asked the girl.

"Whatever."

"What was the other attorney's name?"

"I don't know. I don't pay attention to that stuff."

Though my mother's powers helped keep Tiffany relatively calm, the girl was such a bundle of resentment and entitlement and anger that it kept trickling through everything she said. I was amazed that Tiffany hadn't gotten herself into trouble long before this, considering how unobservant she was.

"Mom, do you have the paperwork they sent you for Tiffany's volunteering here? Since it was court ordered, they had to have sent you something, right?"

"I think your father has it in his office, Charlotte," Mom answered, wiping her hands on her apron.

"Why does the paperwork matter? I don't have to keep volunteering here now that I'm dead, do I? I mean, it seems like the *least* you can do is let me out of *that*." Tiffany crossed her arms.

"The lawyer that represented you when you pled guilty. His name should be somewhere on the paperwork," I told her.

"Why do *you* care who that guy was?"

"Because someone you don't know steered you toward a guilty plea," I explained to her. "It's possible that this was all a set-up just to get you in an isolated area outside of town where you would most likely be alone. Our property isn't in the city limits. It's outside of your dad's direct sphere of control."

"Why would someone do that?"

"To murder you?" I asked her patiently,

though I must admit the conversation felt like one I would have with Samson.

"Oh, right," she sighed. "I'm dead, aren't I? Why hasn't my father shown up yet? I mean, he has to suspect all of you of doing something terrible to me."

"It hasn't been that long, Tiffany, and it's possible the police haven't informed him yet."

"I wouldn't want to be the copper that had to do *that*," she laughed. "He's probably going to get a punch to the mouth just for saying it. Maybe a few before my father actually believes someone would do this to me."

"Why would your father punch a police officer?" Gunther asked, confused.

"Why not?" Tiffany said shrugging. "No one messes with my father. Or me."

I stared at the egocentric, self-involved girl. Her arrogance at her untouchability wasn't even *fazed* by her being dead. Tiffany seemed unable to grasp that someone had, indeed, messed with her and she was beyond her father's protection now.

"We're going to have to close the shelter for a few days so the police can conduct their investigation," my father said as he walked in from the back porch. "I'll put a notice on the website and the social media accounts, though I suspect people will realize we are likely closed once they see the story about the murder in the newspaper."

"Have the police found anything?" I asked my father.

"Well, they suspect she was bashed in the head with one of the paver stones that were behind the kennels, but they haven't found it. We were going to redo the walkway next month." Dad grabbed a drink out of the refrigerator. "Since whoever did this didn't leave the stone, hopefully the murderer still has it. If they find it on someone, it will be good evidence against whoever has it."

"Why would somebody take a bloody paver stone? Ew," I shuddered.

"Fingerprints, maybe? I'm not sure," Dad said and sat down at the table with us. "Obviously, Charlotte, you shouldn't open the circus while you're here. That would just complicate things."

"Wasn't planning on it," I told him. "Did you manage to communicate with the dogs at all? Did they say anything?"

"Unfortunately, they smelled what happened, but they didn't see it happening."

"What do you mean they 'smelled' what happened?" Tiffany asked.

"You moved into the back storeroom behind the curtain. It's across from one of the exits in the building, but both are blocked by the walls. None of the dogs in their kennels would have been able to see what happened in that room, but animals can sense things."

"They sensed my murder?"

"They were alarmed when someone came in, but no dog saw that person walk from their kennel area into the back room, so they would've had to come in through the back exit. There was just something ominous about the person's energy, I suppose. Then they sensed an explosion of aggression, your fear. Of course, once it happened, they smelled the blood as well."

"Ugh, poor dogs," I told him.

"Poor *dogs*? You feel sorry for the *dogs*?" Tiffany spat with indignation. "How about some sympathy for *me*, the newly dead person cut down in the prime of her young, wealthy, privileged life? Daddy was going to buy me a sports car next year! Jeez, you people have your priorities all screwed up."

I stared at the girl.

"Tiffany, to us, the dogs are sentient beings.

Not so different from people, actually," my father explained to her.

"Well, a *little* different from people," I disagreed with my father. "Dogs don't go around bashing people's heads in with paver stones."

"Ugh, whatever. They're just *dogs*. In some countries, they *eat* them, you know," Tiffany told us. "I can't believe everybody gets so hyped up about one dog dying, that I get stuck here and wind up getting bashed in the head. This is *ridiculously* unfair."

"Apparently, your calming power can't turn her into a nice person," I told my mother while ignoring Tiffany's statement.

"Nice people get run over by strong people. Nice is a terrible thing to be. It's *weak*," she told me.

That was it for me. Tiffany Drake was infuriating me, and I let loose.

"Those dogs would have given their *lives* for you. If they could have gotten out of the kennel to save you, they *would* have—even if it cost them their *own* lives," I snapped at her. "Frankly, now that I met you? I'm *glad* they were locked away safe, so no one else was hurt other than you. You are the most spoiled, entitled brat I have *ever* had the unpleasant experience to meet."

"Charlotte!" my mother exclaimed, shocked. "Tiffany is a guest. While I understand how offensive what she is saying is, we don't speak to people that way. I didn't raise you to display such a lack of compassion."

"Compassion for *her*? Where's her compassion for anyone else?" I asked. My mother glared at me.

"Hon, why don't we take a walk?" Gunther got up and leaned next to me to rub my shoulders.

"Hon?" my father asked, stunned.

Gunther froze, his hands wrapped around my shoulders. "You didn't tell them?" he whispered, as if everyone around the table wasn't only two feet away from me.

"They can *hear* you, Gunther," I told him with exasperation. "No. We got interrupted."

"What does this mean?" my mother asked sharply, pointing to Gunther's hands on my shoulders.

"Like I said, we got interrupted with Princess Compassion's murder over there," I told them. "There were still some other things I needed to let you in on. Like Gunther and me."

"You and this young man are dating?" Mom asked.

"Well, it's a little more complicated than that…"

"Oh no! Are you *pregnant*?!" my father asked, horrified.

"No! No, Dad, jeez."

"Mr. Astley—"

"Not a *word*, young man. She may be a ringmaster, but Charlotte is still my daughter. I want to hear this from her," my father told him sternly.

"We both would, Gunther," Mom agreed with a bit more calm in her tone of voice. Despite that, I could see she was shocked. "I'm sure you're a very nice young man, and we mean no disrespect to you, but surely you realize that the two of you having a relationship is the very *definition* of a bad idea."

"We've been in a relationship for a week now, and it hasn't been that bad," I joked. My mother glared at me.

"Do I really need to be here for this? Because frankly, I don't care about any of you," Tiffany said. "You can have your stupid little family whatever without me."

"Can we let her go?" I asked Mom.

"I don't take orders from *you*. Let me know

when my father arrives," she said as she floated up and out of the kitchen window.

"I guess I take orders from her now? Anyway, I probably should go after her," I said as I pushed my chair away from the table and attempted to get the heck out of Dodge before this conversation continued. From my perspective, they knew that I was dating Gunther. Mission accomplished, right?

"Oh no, you don't," Mom said. "Sit back down. She's a ghost. She can't do much damage at the moment. We're going to finish this conversation."

I sighed and sat down.

"*You* can go, young man," my father said as he poked his finger in Gunther's direction.

Gunther looked at me, and I nodded.

My controversial boyfriend leaned over and kissed me on the forehead. Nodding to my parents, he walked out the back door to return to the Magical Midway.

I thought about rubber-banding after him, but figured I was gonna have to have this conversation at some point. May as well be today, a few hours after a girl was murdered in my parents' dog kennels.

Because why not?

Oh, Samson, I miss you right now.

Even though I knew there would be no response, the silence within my own head was deafening.

I'll go check on him while I'm here, Gunther responded in my head. His voice was so clear that it startled me. *Good luck with your parents.*

Are you on the Magical Midway? Like, on the grounds right now?

Yes. I seem to be getting a handle on controlling this telepathy thing.

Well. That was interesting.

Not only could my boyfriend speak to me telepathically, but our telepathic communication powers were also not limited to being on one side of the Magical Midway barrier or the other simultaneously.

I didn't know whether to be excited or alarmed.

CHAPTER 5

"So, I don't think Gunther and I dating is as bad as all that," I finished telling my parents. "We both realize the challenges that come from having a relationship. But he's not a ringmaster yet, so we've got time to try and work it out."

"Well, I'll admit you seem to be well aware of the issues that you face, Charlotte, and I'm impressed with how thoroughly you have both thought this through," Dad said. "I'm glad that the Magical Midway was able to make peace with Roland. He is not a man I would want to be on the wrong side of."

"I do have some questions," my mother said. "Gunther thinks the two of you are fated to be together?"

"Yeah, I know it sounds kind of crazy," I told her. "There's this whole myth around the thirteenth witch of the circuses, and we're both thirteenth generation witches since they started. Ethel Elkins told him since he was a boy that he would marry another thirteenth witch."

"Well, that doesn't necessarily mean it's *you*, Charlotte. The other circus families are still around even if the circuses themselves have disbanded. Surely you're not the *only* two left. The circuses were all founded at the same time so everyone in this generation would have a good chance of being the thirteenth generation witch of their family, wouldn't they?"

My mother brought up a good point I hadn't really considered, and I felt a pang of jealousy for someone I didn't even know existed. If they did, though, she would no doubt be way hotter and less of a pain in the butt than me with my stupid superpower job.

"Maybe. There were a bunch of things that Gunther was told, though, that led him to believe it was me."

"Like what?" my father asked.

"That I would be responsible for leading him to find his place. He figures that was me turning him into a full witch so he could be a ringmaster and a lawgiver," I told him. "That I would bring ideas from the human world, be annoyed at paranormal world corruption. Stuff like that."

"That still very general, Charlotte," Mom said. "The thing about prophecies is they're so generic you can usually make them fit anything you want them to fit. Seers have always frustrated me."

"This did come from a *norn*, Martha. A norn is not just some random seer," my father pointed out.

"Oh, even the norns practice being cryptic, I think," Mom told him. "Do you remember that norn reader that we saw on our honeymoon? The one who saw fur in our future?"

"Well, we *do* operate an animal shelter."

"We do. And if you had taken me to the Werebear Jamboree, that would have been the prediction. If you had bought me a fur coat, *that* would've been the prediction. If we adopted a puppy, that would've fulfilled the prophecy. See what I mean? You can apply it to almost anything."

"I didn't know witches could be skeptics," I observed.

"Have you met your mother?" Dad asked.

"There are some things I'm not skeptical about," Mom said, glaring at Dad. "One of those things is the fact that a ringmaster and a ringmaster heir dating is going to terrify the Witches' Council."

"I think the Witches' Council is already pretty annoyed at both of us, Mom. Considering our plans to challenge the way they run the paranormal world, I don't think they are going to be very fond of us anytime soon, whether we date or not."

"It's more than that," she said, pausing. "I remember hearing a story when I was a little girl about two ringmaster heirs that fell in love years and years ago. It sent the Witches' Council into a panic."

"Do you remember why?" Dad asked her.

"Something about the powers combining. That if two families joined into one, the power they both held was doubled somehow. I wish I could remember more, but I don't."

"What happened to the two people in love? Did they get married?" I asked her.

"No. They were executed. Now, wipe that look off your face, Charlotte," Mom said when she glanced over and spotted my shocked panic. "They were both heirs, not ringmasters. Neither one of them held the power that you have. It is something to be aware of, though. Perhaps it's a good thing Gunther is staying at the Magical Midway."

"That boy has put himself at great risk for you," Dad said with some admiration. "A greater risk than you have put yourself at for him."

"He loves me," I told Dad quietly. My father nodded.

"Do you love him?"

"I don't know," I sighed. "I care about him so much. Whenever something happens, I look around for him. He makes me feel safe, you know? I mean, besides Uncle Phil, he's really the first witch I've known well. And we faced a lot of the same things growing up, feeling different from everybody else."

"He understands you," Mom said.

"I think he does," I told her. "If this were just me and Gunther in the human world I think I'd be drawing doodles of what my name looks like with his last name, you know? But we don't live in the human world, and everything is so much more complicated with the Witches' Council, the circuses, the prophecies. It's harder to know how I feel."

"Charlotte, whether this is a prophecy or not a prophecy, whether the two of you are fated to be together or not fated to be together—none of that affects *love*. Magic can't make someone love someone else. Love is the one thing *no one* can control," Dad told me. "How you feel is simply how you feel, honey."

"If you truly love this boy, you'll know," Mom added. "Love is unmistakable, and it's the most powerful force in the world."

"I swear, you both sound like a Valentine's Day card," I told them.

Mom and Dad laughed.

"I'll try to call more when we're on the road," I promised. "I didn't mean to leave you out, or not tell you about Gunther and me. It was just hectic and the Werebear Jamboree was kind of crazy."

"No problem, honey, we are always here for you," Mom told me warmly. She reached across the kitchen table and squeezed my hand. "I'd like to think on this a while and see if I can remember anything else about the two ringmaster heirs. For now, go with your dad to look at Tiffany's court papers. Let's see who this mystery lawyer was."

"But that's Anthony Drake's attorney. Tiffany was insistent it wasn't the same man, and she was represented by a different attorney," I told my father as we flipped through the court papers. "That's his signature, though. She must be mistaken."

"Look, Charlotte," Dad said as he laid two sets of legal papers next to one another. "The signatures aren't the same. The one on the right signing off on the agreement looks completely different from the one on the left."

"But weren't these filed the same day?"

"No, look at the date," Dad pointed. "This one was filed four days before the hearing. This one? It was signed after."

"Did the police ask you for these?"

"No, but I assume that they have these papers already since they are on file with the court," Dad said.

"Well, it's helpful to establish that she's telling the truth, but not very helpful in figuring out who this guy is," I said as I flipped through the rest of the papers. "After spending some time with her, I have to admit I'm a little daunted by narrowing down who would want her dead. It only took me an hour."

"Took you an hour for what?"

"To want her dead."

"Be glad your mother didn't hear you say that."

"Oh, I don't really mean it," I told him with a sigh. "I just can't believe anyone is that spoiled, or that lacking in human decency that an animal dying because of a prank she pulled doesn't seem to bother Tiffany at all. Not to mention all the other entitled garbage she keeps spouting."

"Tiffany's had quite a hard life. Harder than you would think considering the way she talks about her father," Dad told me. "Her father and mother were not married, and Anthony Drake didn't even know about her until she was ten years old. She faced a great deal of struggle growing up with just her mother, not knowing who her father was. So says the county gossip, in any case."

"So you knew who she was when she came? Didn't you tell Mom?" I asked him while thinking back to my mom's surprise when she realized who Tiffany was.

"Yes, and no. You know your mother. She hates gossip, and I didn't think it was that important," Dad said. "Maybe I should have."

"Is her mother still around?"

"Her mother was hit by a car when she was ten. Her grandparents on her mother's side didn't want her, and the state went looking for her father. I believe she spent a couple of weeks in foster care before they realized her father was Anthony Drake. A DNA test confirmed it. Even though I don't like the man, he *did* take responsibility for the girl. At least that's the story."

"I honestly wonder if she wouldn't have been better off in a foster home," I told him. "She seems to have no empathy, no sense of compassion, no sense of responsibility at all. Considering what I know about her father, she sounds like a chip off the old block."

"I doubt she would have fared any better in a foster home," he disagreed. "She certainly has adopted some of the worst aspects of her father. She's young yet, though. Had she had the chance to live out her adult life, perhaps she would've had the opportunity to change."

"And maybe she would have become a lawyer and carried on the family business of squashing people with trucks for money."

Dad looked as if he wanted to respond, but he shrugged instead.

"I guess it doesn't matter now," I told him, shrugging. "She's dead, so the human world will never get to find out what a stellar human being young Tiffany might have had the ability to grow into."

"Oh, it's worse than that. She's frozen in this moment until she decides to move past it. She is who she will be eternally, unless she breaks free from the issues in her life."

I knew a little about the ghosts, that change for them could be really challenging. I had never looked too deeply into it, but little Anna flashed through my mind. I wondered what issue the little girl could not break free of for five hundred years.

"Wow. That's depressing."

"It is. Which is why I tell you, Charlotte—have some compassion for the girl. You think her life was challenging? Her death will be much more so for her. And she doesn't have her father as a safety net anymore."

I wandered back out toward the kennels, where the police continued to take pictures and measurements of the crime scene. Detective Roberts glanced up at my approach and nodded. I nodded back, and he turned away.

"*Charlotte?*" a shocked voice called from behind me.

As I turned, I expected to see someone from the Magical Midway.

It was not someone from the Magical Midway.

It was my fake ex-boyfriend, Aidan Parker.

"Aidan? What on earth are *you* doing here?"

"Me? *You're* the one that disappeared from the face of the earth!" He laughed as he ran over and embraced me. "When did you get back? I asked your parents how I could get a hold of you, and they said you were off running your family circus and didn't have a cell phone."

"Yeah, no, I never keep it charged," I lied. "We use CB radios on the fairgrounds, so that's what I usually carry."

Or telepathy. A lot of times, we used telepathy.

Aidan looked fantastic. The last time I saw him, he was pale and shaken by the explosion that tore through our little friends circle. Aidan and I were one half of a two-couple group. My best friend Tabitha and Aidan's best friend Bobby were the other half. It was great, and we used to hang out almost every night.

Well, it was great except for one thing.

Aidan and I weren't *really* a couple, Aidan was gay—but he and I didn't tell Tabitha or Bobby.

When the truth came out, all four of us engaged in some spectacular drama, and then went off in four directions never to speak again.

Now? The sadness and tension I saw on his face when we last parted had been replaced. My friend looked relaxed, healthy, and happy.

Good for him.

"I just came by to bring Kyle his lunch," Aidan told me holding a bag up. "He and I have been dating a month or two. Okay, a month and a half. It's pretty new, actually."

"You are dating *him*? The quarterback from my high school football team? You've got to be kidding me!"

"You knew my type was big and tough," Aidan laughed again and nodded. "Come on, don't you think he looks like that movie star we both thought was adorable?"

"If you shave his head, give him a tan, and stick a smile on him occasionally, *maybe*," I told him sarcastically.

Aidan laughed.

"Gosh, Aidan, it's terrific to see you. I was really worried when…Well, you know."

"When my refusal to admit who I am exploded our social lives into epic drama like we were guest stars on a telenovela? It's okay,

Charlotte, it's been almost a year since it happened," Aidan said. "Back then I was really depressed. I mean, *really* depressed. Once I realized I wasn't pulling myself out of it, I got a therapist. She really helped me work through it. Become comfortable with who I am."

"That's good, I'm glad. I'm really happy for you, Aidan."

"Yeah, well, when I finally got my head on straight, I came to see you to apologize, and you had disappeared. Your parents were *kind* of sketchy about why they couldn't get a hold of you. I was worried for a while, but then I just figured it was their polite way of letting me know you didn't want to talk to me."

"That *wasn't* it at all, I promise. Taking over the Magical Midway wasn't a situation that I had a lot of notice about. My Uncle Phil—"

I stopped abruptly in the middle of my story.

How was I supposed to explain to Aidan why I suddenly disappeared to take over the circus? I couldn't tell Aidan that Uncle Phil had died considering it was possible Uncle Phil would stroll out of the Magical Midway at any moment. I couldn't explain cell phones were banned because GPS could track us moving across the country in the blink of an eye.

"Charlotte? You okay?"

"Yeah, I just…It was a family thing. It's kind of complicated, so let's just leave it at that. In any case, I didn't have much notice that I was going to have to leave. I would've called you before I left, but…"

I was teleported, Aidan, and I had no time to pick up the phone.

"You thought I didn't want to talk to you, didn't you?"

"Yep, that was *exactly* it," I lied. "We all just scattered to the wind. I figured you were going through a lot more than I was, so I just left you alone, figuring you would contact me when you were ready. After I started traveling with the circus, honestly, I just didn't have a lot of time to think of home."

"Aidan, what are you doing here?" Detective Roberts asked sharply as he walked up to us.

"Hi!" Aidan smiled warmly at the detective. "I saw the midday news and figured you might be here a while. Since I'm intimately familiar with how out-of-the-way this place is, I brought you lunch."

Detective Roberts grabbed the bag from Aidan's hand, and murmured a thank you that was anything but warm. I bristled at the distracted way Kyle Roberts was treating Aidan, and his lack of gratitude. I sensed annoyance flowing off the burly detective.

"Next time, call first," he said, holding up the bag. "Appreciate it though. I have to get back to work."

"Right, right, sorry. I didn't mean to interrupt," Aidan responded. Disappointment trickled from him. Images of him and Kyle eating lunch together flashed in my head as Aidan moved his hand to hide his own lunch bag behind his hip. "Will I see you tonight?"

"Maybe," Kyle grunted, and turned away. Aidan watched him go.

"So, that…That's your boyfriend?"

"That's my something," Aidan said, and sighed. "I don't think I'm very good at this."

"Well, it *is* a murder scene. Maybe he was just distracted?"

"That's kind of you to say, Charlotte, but you've always been pretty intuitive. You and I *both* know that wasn't just Kyle being distracted," he said.

"Is he the first guy that you've gone out with since coming out?"

"Is it *that* obvious?"

"Come on." I grabbed his hand. "Let me show

you around the circus. No one can stay sad or troubled at a circus."

At least no human could.

Unfortunately for us paranormals, the circus atmosphere wasn't quite as carefree.

Aidan nodded, and we walked toward my nomadic magical home.

CHAPTER 6

JUST BEFORE WE CROSSED THE INVISIBLE BOUNDARY into the Magical Midway, Aidan jumped.

"What's wrong?" I asked him.

"I, um, I don't know, actually." Aidan patted his hands against his head. "It almost felt like a bee stung me on my scalp, but I don't feel anything. No bumps. And the pain is gone now. Well, mostly gone."

I stopped walking and examined Aidan's now pale skin. Beads of sweat stood out suddenly on his brow, and his hands shook ever so slightly.

"You know, let's go back to my parents' house instead," I told him as I steered him away from the circus. "They have air conditioning that's much more powerful than the fans I have in my tent. I can show you the circus later."

Aidan nodded and followed me up the path toward the house as I wracked my brain through our past. I couldn't remember Aidan telling me anything about being psychic, or intuitive, or having any interest in any paranormal anything.

And yet when he got two feet from the Magical Midway border, he felt *something*.

"You're looking a little better," I told him. The further away we walked from the circus the more color returned to Aidan's cheeks. The shaking in his hands slowed, and his forehead slowly dried in the hot Texas breeze.

"It must be the promise of air conditioning," he responded, smiling. "I never did get used to being outside in these hot Texas summers. I'm probably just dehydrated."

"So, let's get back to you and the hunky detective." We climbed the steps to my parents' back porch. "Is he always that grumpy?"

"I know he has a tough job, you know? Seeing people murdered and dealing with dead bodies and people that kill. I mean, I couldn't do that kind of job day after day," he told me, holding the back door open. "But I just can't seem to get past his super tough, suspicious armor. Sometimes I wonder why he bothered going out with me in the first place."

"He bothered because you're handsome, kind, smart and would be a great catch for anyone. Obviously, he sees that, even if he doesn't act like it."

"Doesn't act like what?" My father joined us in the kitchen. "Aidan! What are you doing here? With all the tragedy this morning I forgot to tell Charlotte you had stopped by to see her."

"Mr. Astley," Aidan nodded. "My...a friend of mine is working on Tiffany Drake's case. When I heard it happened out here and that there was a big circus next to the shelter, I took a chance and headed over."

"Well, I'm sure Charlotte is glad you came by," Dad told him while shaking his hand. "Have you taken a tour of the Magical Midway yet?"

"We were just about to, but I got overheated, I think," Aidan responded as his hand rubbed over the part of his skull that had pained him. "I thought I was stung by something, and I felt a bit woozy when we walked over there. It was pretty weird, too, because there's no swelling on my head. Probably a phantom pain from being dehydrated."

Dad looked at me sharply.

"Hopefully, we won't be here that long," I told my father. "I can give him a tour the next time we swing into town."

"I really want to see it, though, Charlotte! I just need to sit in the air conditioning and drink some water."

Mom came in and greeted Aidan. With the two chatting, Dad pulled me into the hallway.

"Did you cross the barrier with him?" Dad whispered.

"No," I shook my head. "I think we were about two feet from crossing when he suddenly felt like he'd been stung. I take it you're thinking the same thing I'm thinking? That he might be paranormal?"

"Clearly, it's a possibility, Charlotte," Dad said, thinking. "There's no other reason he would be sensitive to the Magical Midway energy unless he were descended from a witch. If he were a known paranormal, he would know what the Magical Midway is. You would've sensed it by now."

"I can't let him onto the Magical Midway."

"Clearly not, but you don't think that's going to cause some suspicion? Isn't he friends with the detective? If you don't bring him into the grounds, he may tell his friend. It will look like we're hiding something."

"Aidan wouldn't do that."

"Not on *purpose*, Charlotte. What may not seem suspicious to your friend Aidan could seem very suspicious to his detective friend."

I looked at my friend sitting at our kitchen table. Less than a year ago, his lie caused our lives to explode. I wondered if my lie was the new ticking time bomb.

"Maybe it's not what we think it is," I told my dad.

"Charlotte, you don't solve anything by pretending that reality is not what it is," Dad warned me. "Your friend's power began awakening just being near the paranormal border. Aidan is part witch, and he found his way to the Magical Midway. You have to decide whether to trust the intuition that guided him to that border, or to step in between him and that pull and block him from a world that is, at least in part, his."

"And I have to do it without being able to tell him anything," I bitterly told my father. "How do you make a decision like that for someone? Decide that when you can't even ask them what they would want?"

"I don't know. I don't envy you."

Regardless of what I decided, the risks were mounting in every direction.

Gunther, can you hear me?

Yes, Charlotte. Everything okay?

Aidan is a paranormal.

Wait, what? How do you know this? This is your friend from Mickwac, right? The fake boyfriend you had?

Yes, that's him, I told him. *He showed up here. I was bringing him to the Magical Midway to show him the circus. He reacted to the boundary. My dad and I are pretty sure that he's a paranormal.*

*That's...*Gunther's telepathic message trailed off as he considered the implications of what I had told him. *That complicates the situation, but not incredibly so.*

Aidan is dating Detective Kyle Roberts.

Okay, that's a significant complication.

I know it is.

How can I help?

I don't know, I told him. *I just wanted to tell you.*

I felt a warmth flow from the direction of the Magical Midway to me. It was like a soft, pink hug, and I took comfort from it.

Since Gunther and I had committed to making the relationship work, it seemed as if our bond had strengthened, and the powers that connected us grew more powerful. The connection, once nothing more than memories of him in my mind, had metamorphosed into a keen tie between us.

The strapping detective opened the back door and walked into our kitchen without asking. Aidan looked up at the rugged man and smiled hesitantly, but Detective Roberts stared back at him and frowned.

"I guess when you work in small towns and rural areas at some point you get a case where everyone knows everyone else," Detective Roberts said. "I can't say that this isn't a bit awkward, though."

"Aidan and I were close friends long before he ever started dating you," I responded a little defensively. Who did this guy think he was? "I'm sorry if the fact that he's here is making you uncomfortable. I can't see why it would."

"This whole case is making me a little uncomfortable," the detective responded. He pulled up a chair at the kitchen table without asking. "It seems to me that with visitors to the shelter, and entire circus within eyeshot of the kennel area, and the entire family that works at the shelter sitting at the window, someone should have seen something."

"Is it your experience that murderers often go out of their way to be seen, Detective?" I asked him. I probably should have just kept my mouth shut, but the way Kyle was treating Aidan had gotten on my nerves.

"It's my experience that murderers aren't that smart, Charlotte," Detective Roberts responded. "This one took the murder weapon, left no footprints, wasn't on any of the cameras, and wasn't seen by anyone. That's either someone *very* lucky or very experienced in hiding their crimes. Or…"

"Or?" Aidan asked.

"Or someone's covering for the murderer," Kyle Roberts stared directly at me.

"And you think that because…?" I stared the detective in the eye.

"Honestly? Because it's one of the options," he responded, shrugging. "To be honest, none of you strike me as guilty. Though your arrival here, Charlotte, has some ridiculously odd timing. But I don't think you did it."

"While I appreciate that, I'm curious as to why?"

"When you walked out toward the back you were within feet of the dog kennels," Kyle said. "Not one of them reacted aggressively. None of them even looked concerned. Unless you have some magical dog power to make them all not bark at you when you're a murderer, if you *had* killed that girl those dogs would have reacted. Your parents have been well-known around here for years. I don't think they would've covered for you. Not for this."

"Well, thank you for your trust in our honesty, Detective," my father said as he entered. "We may not have been fond of the girl, but we certainly didn't want to see her dead."

"I don't think you have anything to hide deliberately," the detective responded. "But I still think it could've been someone else on the circus grounds."

"Well, if you believed I didn't kill her because of the dogs' reaction, there's an easy way to prove if anyone did," I told him.

"Oh?"

"Have everyone walk through the kennels. See if any of the dogs alert on anyone."

"How would I know you had everyone walk through?" Kyle asked me.

"I thought you just said I have nothing to hide?" I asked him.

"Forgive me for being a little bit suspicious after you told me carnie people don't trust the cops," Kyle said with a wry grin. "Are you going to hand over your entire list of employees so I can check each one?"

"Some people own their own joints, Detective. I wouldn't have their list of employees."

If I handed over a list of people to the detective and he performed any kind of background check, he would discover in short order that a good portion of them just don't exist in the human world. I couldn't provide him with the information he would need to clear my people.

Because, um, most of them weren't people.

"Then we're back to square one. It would take a lot of time to set up, and I couldn't even be sure that we got everybody. While I appreciate the suggestion, I think I'm going to have to do good old-fashioned detective work to figure this out."

"Do you have any leads or directions you're looking into?" my mother asked him.

"The elephant in the room is that Tiffany Drake is the daughter of Anthony Drake. I think now that we've wrapped up gathering evidence here, I need to start poking around Mr. Drake's enemy list. I also need to learn a little bit more about Tiffany herself."

"That enemy list? That could be a very long list," my mother observed.

Detective Roberts nodded.

"Are we free to go if we get a job somewhere else, Detective?" I asked.

"So soon? Charlotte, we've barely had any time to talk!" Aidan protested. "At least stay a couple of days so we can catch up. I don't know anything about your life anymore, and I could…I could use some…"

"Some movie nights and popcorn like the old days?" I finished for Aidan since I knew for sure what he was trying to say. He needed advice on Detective Kyle Roberts.

"Absolutely," he nodded.

"Maybe for a couple of days," I told him.

"It would help if you stayed around," the detective added. "I'd prefer that nothing about the crime scene change too much if we can possibly avoid it."

Even though we were not suspects anymore, I could see that the folks who worked in my circus could potentially move to the top of Detective Roberts' suspect list relatively quickly.

We still needed to solve the case to protect the circus.

We also needed to figure out what, exactly, we would do with Tiffany Drake. I did not want to bring the girl with us.

The police left the property, the handsome Detective Kyle Roberts going with them. Aidan stood at the front window watching the cars pull away.

"Okay, he's gone," I said as I stepped up next to him. "He seems a little mercurial, and I definitely sensed that he wasn't the friendliest guy you could've wound up with. But he seems like a good person."

"He is a good person," Aidan agreed. Turning away from the window he sat down on the couch in my parents' living room. "I just don't know what our relationship is, you know? Are we dating? Is he dating other people? Is he my boyfriend?"

"Have you just asked him?"

"Well, no," my friend responded somewhat sheepishly. "Honestly, Charlotte, I don't even know how to ask him. I think I'm afraid if I ask him, I won't get the answer that I want."

"What answer do you want?"

"I don't know."

I stared at Aidan and raised my eyebrow.

"Yeah, I know. It doesn't make any sense," he laughed.

"Look, you and I didn't have a wide circle of friends, and we both had some challenges in the trust department," I told him. "If you're not even comfortable enough to talk to him about your relationship, it doesn't seem like this relationship has much of a chance."

Aidan nodded, and I sensed a sadness and loneliness in him.

"Aidan, do you even really like this guy?"

He looked surprised at the question, but I didn't sense any shock from my friend. Shrugging, Aidan's fingers toyed with a frayed rip in his jeans. "He's a really nice guy," he said finally.

"Oh my gosh, Aidan! There can be lots of really nice guys that you don't fall for! He's cute, and he's nice, but do you 'like him' like him?"

"Why wouldn't I?"

Aidan's problem came into perfect clarity. He felt like he should fall for the handsome detective. Kyle Roberts was good-looking, he was nice, he had a heroic job. Despite the fact that Kyle was a heckuva catch, Aidan simply didn't have chemistry with him.

But he wanted to. So much. After so many years alone, though, he was trying to force it.

"Aidan, you don't have to marry the first guy that's interested in you—"

Aidan's face turned white, and he stared across the room toward the doorway. His hands began to shake ,and he pressed hard into the back of the sofa as if he wanted to disappear.

"What is that? What is that? What the heck is that!" he whispered.

I turned and looked at the doorway.

I saw the ghost of Tiffany Drake staring back.

"What are you seeing, Aidan?" I asked him, as fear gripped my innards. I was almost sure I knew what he was going to say, and it was the last thing I wanted to hear.

"Can't you see it? It's the dead girl, isn't it? That's her! I saw her picture on the news! But it can't be," Aidan gasped out the words. "I can see right through her! What the heck is going on?"

"I have a name, jerk," Tiffany responded.

Aidan's eyes widened as his breath caught.

Then his head flopped over as he passed out.

"Great. Now two people are dead! I swear, this stupid place is cursed," Tiffany told me.

I didn't disagree with her.

CHAPTER 7

"WELL, I SHOULD'VE REALIZED IF HE WAS descended from a witch that he would probably be able to see a ghost," I told my family as we frantically discussed what to do.

"You think so, Charlotte?" my uncle asked sarcastically.

"Can't we wipe his memory?" my mother wondered.

"Not without taking him to the Magical Midway and having Charlotte do it," my father said. "Once we take him there, his powers will fully awaken and who knows *what* those will be."

"It's a catch twenty-two." I sighed. "We take him there, and he becomes a half-witch. We don't take him there, and we have to come up with some explanation for what he saw."

"Can we drug him?" Uncle Phil asked.

"I am *not* drugging Aidan. Don't be ridiculous."

"That boy is not going to stay passed out forever. I suggest that someone come up with something," Uncle Phil said. "My vote is for drugs. Don't humans take them for all sorts of reasons?"

"Aidan doesn't do drugs," I told him. "Besides, we would have to give him some type of hallucinogenic drug to make him think what he saw was all in his head. Not only doesn't Aidan do drugs, but even if he did, no one is gonna do it in the middle of an afternoon."

"I'm sure some people do," Uncle Phil said.

"Let's drop the drug option, okay? Not gonna happen."

"Can we just pretend he was imagining it and ignore it?" my mother asked.

"That's an idea, Martha, but that also assumes that Tiffany Drake will stay out of sight for the rest of the time Aidan is visiting us. Do we really want to bank on the girl following directions? She didn't do that very well when she was alive."

"You know, I can *hear* you, Mr. Astley," Tiffany called from behind my father.

"No offense meant, dear," my mother called back.

"Bite me, old woman," Tiffany responded. Mom rolled her eyes.

"I think counting on Tiffany to stay out of sight should be discarded as an option," my father told us as he coughed. His hand went distractedly to the gray hair at his temple.

"You know, Charlotte, swinging by to visit your parents? *Stellar* idea. Truly. I have to commend you," Uncle Phil murmured quietly.

"How the heck was I supposed to know that some spoiled brat was going to get a paver stone to the head two hours after we landed? Or that one of my closest human friends was secretly a paranormal? Or that a football player that sat behind me in some high school class was a detective? Cut me some slack, Uncle Phil. This one's not on me."

"One of your friends is a paranormal?" Fiona asked as she and Ningul made their way down the hallway. "Fancy *that*. We're just finding new witches all over the place!"

"I didn't bring him across the barrier, but we came close," I told her. "Too close. I think the barrier is getting…I don't know, like, it's reaching out further. We were a couple of feet away so it shouldn't have awakened *anything* in him. But Aidan saw Tiffany's ghost."

"That's Aidan?" Fiona asked, pointing to my friend passed out on the couch.

"Yep."

"Why is he sleeping?"

"He passed out. I guess in shock from seeing a ghost for the first time."

"Humans don't pass out for very long, do they? Not as long as you people usually argue over what to do, in any case."

Aidan stirred and lifted his head, blinking. His eyes scanned us talking in the hallway, and then drifted back to Tiffany standing at the front window.

"I must be dreaming," he whispered, his hands shaking again.

"Well, if you are maybe I'll get lucky and be dreaming, too," Tiffany snapped at him. "Because I don't particularly want to be a ghost any more than you want to see one, handsome."

"Okay, we need a plan," I said as I turned back to the group.

"Tell him," Gunther said as he appeared behind Fiona and Ningul.

"Are you *crazy*? We'd be breaking the rule if he stays human."

"A rule you don't even agree with, Charlotte," Gunther pointed out.

"Young man, she *cannot* tell him the truth," my mother told him sternly. "It would put us all in danger."

"We are *already* in danger. Everyone here has been since the moment Charlotte became ringmaster. With all due respect, ma'am, Charlotte knows her friend. It's Charlotte's choice to make. And forgive me for saying so but it is a choice she would not have had to make if you both had not rejected the paranormal world."

My mother stared at Gunther in shock at as the rest of the group turned and faced me expectantly.

"No," I told them after considering all the options. "It's not my choice to make. It's Aidan's."

My mother, father, and uncle all protested at once.

"Charlotte, you can't—"

"The rule is the most important—"

"Are you daft, girl—"

"Aidan is *who he is*," I told them as I cut them all off. "He *deserves* to know who he is. He deserves to make the choice."

"What if he chooses wrong? What if you give him all this knowledge and then he betrays us?" my father asked.

"Then I will take him across the border and allow the magic to awaken his powers," I responded slowly. "And after that, I will turn him into a human. If I can turn a half-witch into a full witch, Roland and I *have* to be able to turn a half-witch into a full human. But at least it will be *his* choice to accept or reject who he is. With everyone hiding from the police, no one will even know."

The faces of my friends and family mirrored the shock and horror of one another's reactions. None had realized Roland and I would have this power, and the idea that we might be able to strip a paranormal of who and what they were horrified them.

It never occurred to them we could take as easily as we could give. Now they did, and it frightened each and every one.

But they nodded.

"Daddy! My Daddy's here!" Tiffany shouted. "Daddy! Daddy, I'm here!"

"You have to be kidding me," I told everyone assembled in the hall. "I swear, we can't seem to catch a break."

We all moved back into the living room. Aidan woke up and footsteps echoed from the front stairs. My human friend, maybe not entirely as human as I thought, continued to stare at the glowing ghost with a shocked expression of horror.

"I know this is freaking you out," I told him. "But I need you to just hold your questions until we get Anthony Drake out of the house. Aidan, that's Fiona and Ningul. They're friends of mine from the circus. Go with them."

Aidan stared at me and then moved his gaze to them. His eyes drifted slowly back, but he didn't move from the couch.

"Aidan, come on, please?"

He was in shock. He didn't move.

"We'll sit with him, Charlotte," Fiona said.

"Let me sit on one side," Gunther said and scrambled over to the couch. "I can't do anything permanently, but I can settle him down if he starts freaking out."

"I can handle his emotions, Gunther, if you can be ready to silence his voice," my mother told him. She moved toward the chair next to the couch. Gunther nodded as he sank into the cushions next to Aidan.

Poor Aidan. I'd never seen him look as overwhelmed as he did at that moment. The good thing was that his reaction of fight or flight or freeze? He fell on the side of freeze. As long as he *stayed* that way, we should be able to focus on Anthony Drake.

A loud and insistent knock echoed from the door.

"Just a minute!" I called from the living room. I took one last glance around for no other reason than to make myself feel better.

With a gangster standing on the welcome mat, a ghost standing at the window, and my friend Aidan frozen in a panic on the couch, while my mother and boyfriend shoved elements of psychic control around him like he was a wild calf to be lassoed…frankly, I wasn't sure the situation could get any more complicated.

Never think that things can't get more complicated, Charlotte, Gunther thought. *They always can, and it seems lately that they surely do.*

I didn't bother responding.

Upon opening the door, I came face-to-face with a furious Anthony Drake. The man looked like a gangster right off a Hollywood mafia movie set. The thick scent of a woodsy cologne cascaded over me as if the man had the power of offensive magic.

I sneezed.

"Are you one of the *idiots* that runs this place?" he growled at me as he leaned forward aggressively. "The police told me that my little girl was murdered this morning. I want to see where it happened. I want to know what you know about *what happened to my daughter.*"

"Mr. Drake, I think we should perhaps deal with the situation a bit more delicately than usual," a tall, pale-looking gentleman stated from behind him. "My apologies, Miss, I'm sure you can understand that Mr. Drake has had a tough day and is in quite a state."

"Of course," I responded. "This is been a pretty traumatic day for everyone."

"No one more so than *my daughter*, you twit," the hulking man growled at me again.

"Mr. Drake, I totally understand that the loss of your daughter in such tragic circumstances is a difficult issue to deal with emotionally. Please know that we're here to help you in any way that we can. It will be easier to help you, though, if you understand that we are not responsible for what happened to your daughter."

"Oh yeah? How do I know that!"

"Mr. Drake, sir, Detective Roberts did let you know that none of the owners of the animal shelter are under suspicion," the mousy man said in a quiet voice. The man following Anthony Drake like a puppy rested a gentle hand on the big man's shoulder. He spoke quietly, even soothingly, to the solidly muscled gangster. I had seen enough movies to assume this was likely his body man, but I thought body men were bigger and more robust than this guy seemed to be.

Anthony Drake stomped across the living room and stared outside the window. The same window that his daughter's ghost stared out of.

The two merged into one with a shimmer at the shoulder.

As much as Tiffany Drake had been obnoxious, demanding, and had subjected us to a near constant stream of complaints and demands, my heart broke for her. With her father sharing the same space as her specter, I could sense the first tendrils of grief wrapping around her as her father's eyes cast through the space she occupied without seeing her.

"Daddy, can you see me?" Tiffany whispered as she looked up into the face of the scariest man in Mickwac. "Daddy, I'm right *here*. I'm right here, Daddy."

Aidan's panicked face softened with sympathy for the girl. For the first time since any of us had met her, Tiffany Drake was a vulnerable, sad, grief-stricken young woman. Despite what she had done and despite how she had acted, no one in the room could be unmoved by her heartrending words to the father who would never hear them again.

"My name is Michael Hayden," the quiet man said. He stepped forward and extended his hand. "I am Mr. Drake's assistant, and I again apologize for his rudeness. As I said, it's been a trying day. Mr. Drake would appreciate if you would allow him to see the location where his daughter lost her life. He would also like to ask you all some questions. In case anyone has any information that they were perhaps uncomfortable sharing with the police."

"I'm not sure what you mean, Mr. Hayden. We told the police everything that we know," my father told the man.

"No one tells those idiots *everything* that they know," Anthony Drake snorted.

"We'd be happy to show you where it happened, if that's what you'd like," I responded.

"What I'd like is to snap the neck of the idiot that was dumb enough to think he could get away with murdering my daughter," Anthony Drake proclaimed. He turned around and stared angrily at me. "And make no mistake, I'll find out who did this long before the police. If I'm feeling generous *maybe* I'll text them and let them know where the body is."

"Of course, this is all hyperbole," Michael Hayden jumped in and grabbed Anthony Drake's arm. "Mr. Drake is in a highly emotional state, and nothing that he's saying should be taken at face value. He is simply a grieving father and is expressing anger the way any grieving father would."

"Oh, is that what that was?" Fiona murmured. Ningul grabbed her hand and squeezed it quickly. "I get it, I get it. No need to break my fingers, there, sweetheart."

My family and friends seemed to sense the danger that radiated off of Anthony Drake. Even the ones that didn't have inherent powers. My father and I caught each other's eyes a few times as we all moved toward the back door. Everyone gave the hyperbolic grieving father a wide space.

There was absolutely no reason for the entire group to move out the back door and toward the dog kennels. One person could have led the two men to the isolated area where Tiffany Drake lost her life. With no discussion, though, it seemed we all decided no one should be alone with the two men.

Even Aidan got up to follow.

Anthony Drake was a dangerous man seemingly incapable of subterfuge at the moment. The gentle seeming Michael Hayden?

As he placed a guiding hand on Anthony Drake's elbow, I gasped in pain. A flash of pure hatred cut through my brain. It was so intense, so sharp and focused that my eyes cast about wildly trying to determine where this dark fury had come from.

After a few moments of scanning each person ambling toward the kennel in silence, my eyes settled on the unassuming man that walked just to the right of and slightly behind Anthony Drake.

I was sure that it came from Michael Hayden.

"Are you all right?" Gunther asked quietly. We walked slowly in the middle of the group. We weren't five feet down the path that led to the kennels before Anthony Drake stepped in front of us and led the way as if he had been here before. He hadn't, not that I ever remembered.

"Yeah, I just felt something I wasn't expecting to feel," I told him quietly. "This whole situation is making me jumpy, I guess."

"I would've thought you would be jumpy *long* before this," he told me.

"When people die and turn into sparkle ash it doesn't make you as jumpy as when they die and bleed all over the floor," I retorted. "Actually, it's not even that. The...world that we live in? It's more serious and less serious to me, I guess. Somehow all of this feels *more* real. Somehow. It shouldn't, but it does."

"Here we are, Mr. Drake." My father stepped around the pair and held the door for them politely. "Tiffany was working in here this morning. If you just walk through the kennels behind the curtain at the end of the hall? That's where..."

Anthony Drake stared daggers at my father before pushing past him.

"I can't believe he can't see or hear me," Tiffany whined. "What am I even still a ghost for if I can't talk to my father? He fixes everything. If you can't hear me, Daddy, and you can't fix *anything*, why am I stuck here? How am I supposed to move on? They don't expect me to do it myself, do they?"

I didn't know whether Tiffany was speaking to herself, her father, or us. Unfortunately, with two criminal human beings in our group, none of us would answer.

Not that we *could* answer. We were paranormals, not gods. I had no clue why she hadn't moved on.

Our lack of reaction to her questions and complaints did not sit well with her, and Tiffany's whining became more insistent. I wondered if I could send her somewhere the way I shoved the Witches' Council back where they came from.

I probably *could*, but it was against the law.

I think, anyway.

The scraggly brown mutt in the first kennel growled at the two men, saliva dripping from its maw. His muscles were tense, haunches flexing. The accusatory stare from the gangster did nothing to dissuade the canine from his aggressive stance.

Anthony Drake jumped toward the front gate and kicked the metal cage with a fury. The dog yelped as he dropped his tail and slunk to the back of his enclosure.

"Daddy hates dogs," Tiffany told no one in particular.

"Of course he does," my mother sighed.

"I didn't hurt the stupid animal!" Mr. Drake shouted at her. "I don't need to hear these mangy mouths echoing in my ears as I visit the place that my daughter drew her last breath! They should have a little respect!"

Well, now we know where she got it, Gunther thought to me.

The kennel contained large cages on either side, living quarters for the dogs waiting for their forever homes. Those dogs that had come in with a friend got to stay with them, and so the twelve enclosures held fifteen dogs.

Fifteen frightened dogs. The little Chihuahua to the right of me shook like a leaf. Dark, liquid eyes stared from the back of his living quarters in fear. It was a posture I would see again and again as we walked.

It wasn't normal.

Jeez, Gunther, all the dogs are terrified of him, I thought back.

I don't blame them. We're all a little jumpy, too. I think between us being nervous and his attack on the enclosure gate, the animals are just reacting to the energy in here. He is a gangster, after all. Maybe they're just responding to him as a person.

"Stupid girl," Anthony Drake whispered as he jerked open the curtain. "All for a stupid sorority prank. You stupid, *stupid* little girl. I always told you rule number one is to *not get caught*. Maybe it was better that someone got you *now* rather than years down the line when you could've pulled me *down with you*."

We were all stunned.

I expected some kind of fatherly outburst of mourning, some grief, maybe even a single manly tear down his bristled cheek.

But a tongue-lashing for his dead daughter's actions?

What a selfish narcissist. The words were painful to listen to. It was even more painful to watch the spoiled ghost's reaction.

As much as Fiona disliked the girl, her face cracked in sympathy as she moved in front of Tiffany. Facing the girl, her hands, hidden by her body, moved frantically to motion out of Anthony's sight. The kelpie was trying to convince Tiffany to leave.

The pretty girl's apparition remained motionless, held captive by the angry image of her father and his words.

"You were going to be the queen of my empire, you *stupid* child. You and Michael. Not only could you not get caught, but you also weren't even tough enough *not to be killed.*"

"Mr. Drake, this is completely inappropriate—"

"What do you *care*?" Anthony Drake roared, whirling on my father. "She's *dead*. It's not like the idiot girl can *hear* me anymore," he snapped. "Your family has lived here a long time. You *know* who I am. Since you know who I am, you know who she *should have been*. But that's her blood, so clearly she *wasn't who she should have been.*"

"I can't believe you're saying this about your own daughter," I snapped at him. "No one deserves to be killed! No one is responsible for their own murder!"

"Oh, I believe that some people *do*, Ms. Astley," Michael Hayden disagreed quietly. "Some people *do* deserve to be killed. Some people bring the hand within mortal striking distance by their own actions."

"Considering what the two of you do and who you are, it doesn't surprise me to hear you say that. Out here in the real world, though, people don't use murder as a way to settle a score."

"The real world?" Hayden responded, amused.

The wiry man turned and stepped toward me with an out-sized dignity and pride considering his words. "The real world is a cold, heartless place where people struggle and only the strong survive. The strong, and those that are weak who have someone strong to protect them."

Michael Hayden was a sheet of glass. Poking around the corners of his mind and emotions I could only sense myself reflecting back at me. The man was disciplined, cold.

"However, we didn't come here to discuss the inequities in the world," he continued. "We came to see the place where the girl fell."

Michael Hayden gestured with an open palm to the corner, eyes lingering over the puddle of dried blood that stained the concrete floor.

"Now we have."

"She knew," Aidan said as if in a hazy dream. "Her eyes rose and met the killer's cold stare. She knew as she saw him approach." He swayed on his feet, and Gunther grabbed his arm to hold him steady. "She didn't know why. She didn't realize he knew it was all because of him."

"What is he talking about? What does he mean?" Anthony Drake barked.

"Mr. Drake, I don't think there's anything more to be learned here," Michael Hayden told him calmly. "Clearly these people are simply a bunch of do-gooders that don't have anything more to share with us."

"You're probably right, Michael," Drake agreed and turned his back on the place where his daughter had died. "At least I have you. It's a shame that no one of my blood was smart enough to grab what I could have given them. Stupid women. Their mothers…I always had a weakness for stupid women. You did the best you could for her, Michael, I'm sure."

Anthony Drake babbled as Michael Hayden attempted to lead him away.

"Yes, Mr. Drake," Michael Hayden responded.

I had never wanted to clobber someone so much in my entire life. Anthony Drake was a repugnant human being. Tiffany Drake didn't have a chance of turning into a decent person with a father like this.

"If anything else happens, you call me." Anthony Drake ordered us. He jabbed his fat finger in our direction. "You get me? Don't call the police. You call *me*. Me or Michael. Me or Michael only. Understand?"

"Please let us know if you need anything else," I told him through clenched teeth, refusing to agree to his demands. "I trust you can see yourself out?"

"Women," the man murmured, turning on his heel. "Can't live with them, can't shoot them. Well, can't shoot a lot of them or the police get suspicious."

"Yes, Mr. Drake," Hayden responded.

Michael Hayden paused at the exit to the kennel and turned back to meet my eyes. With a sharp nod, he followed his boss out.

CHAPTER 8

"WHY IS HE *LEAVING*? WHY ARE YOU LETTING HIM leave? He was just angry, that's how Daddy deals with things." Tiffany moved toward the door with her glowing hands outstretched. The young woman's voice was rough, as she wrestled with her love for her horrible father and the things she had just heard him say about her.

"Tiffany, your father won't be able to see you, so there's nothing he can do to help you," I told her. "*We'll* help you. I promise. Just forget about your father for now."

I admit, what I said was somewhat cold. Although I had my issues with my parents and my uncle, I had never seen a parent so cruel to a child before. Even an adult child. Even though I had sympathy for her, Tiffany's allegiance to the awful gangster baffled me. And it bothered me.

Why do people show dedication to others— even when those others are just out to abuse them? I saw it with the Witches' Council repeatedly, and I was watching it with Tiffany and Anthony Drake.

Charlotte, all people are more complicated than they seem, Gunther said in my mind. *Whatever else he is, he is still her father. She loves him, and we are strangers to her. It's not surprising, even after what he said, that she would be pained by his leaving.*

If my father treated me like that, there's no way I would be walking after him with that lost little waif look on my ghost face.

Gunther didn't respond, but I could feel his emotional discomfort with my judgment. I shrugged it off and turned back to Tiffany. I didn't have time to explain myself to my boyfriend.

And frankly, I didn't feel like I should have to. How could he not get it?

"Forget about him? How can I forget about him? That man has controlled my life since I was ten years old. I don't know how to live without Daddy telling me what I need to do."

I'm not supposed to be judgmental? Really?

I bit my tongue.

"Well, it's a good thing you're not alive then, dear," my mother told her, smiling. "You are your *own* ghost now, and you can decide what type of ghost you would like to be."

"What does that mean?" she asked, puzzled.

"We can't help you move on," I told her. "We are all alive. We don't know what that means, really. Moving on, what happens after people die or after their ghost disappears. It's still a mystery."

"Speak for yourself," Uncle Phil said, offended. "I'm not alive."

"But you have a body," Tiffany said, still confused.

"I do, but I'm not alive," he told her.

"So, do *you* know what moving on means? Aren't I supposed to get some big house in heaven and all sorts of rewards and riches because of who Daddy was?"

"I'm almost positive that's not how it works," Uncle Phil told her.

"Well, *how* does it work, then?"

"I don't know. I said I was dead, not omniscient."

"What does that word mean?"

"He saying he's not a know-it-all," I told her. "Although I have to tell you, I could bring up a few discussions he and I have had that would argue that assertion."

"He was just trying to help you. Even when he sounded arrogant, he was scared, and was trying to help," Aidan said in that soft and dreamy voice. "He was frightened for you, frightened by what was going on. He didn't want you to know he was frightened. He projected strength, hoping that by projecting strength for you, you wouldn't be afraid…"

"Okay, what the *heck* is going on with him?" I asked. "What is this?"

"Oh, oh, I think I know," my mother said, shocked. "It's retrocognition. I've heard about this power. It's *very* rare."

"Retrocognition?"

"Well, *everyone* has heard of precognition, correct?" my mother asked. A few of us nodded. "This is the companion talent to precognition. With *pre*cognition, you can see an incident or glimpses of an incident that will likely take place in the future. With *retro*cognition, you can see an event of the past. Some people even believe that humans who see ghosts are simply experiencing a form of retrocognition surrounding an event. It's a specific type of clairvoyance."

"But there *are* ghosts," Tiffany pointed out. "I

mean, I'm here, right? Wait a minute—am I not here?"

"There are usually multiple explanations, paranormal and otherwise, for the things humans can see but can't explain. Not all ghosts are ghosts, but some are. Nothing to worry about, dear."

"So we now have the past, present, and future covered," Gunther laughed. "I guess that could be handy."

My head snapped on my neck at Gunther's observation. What he said tickled some buried memory deep inside my mind I couldn't entirely access.

"Say that again? What do you mean?"

"Well, *you* can peek into people's present. Whether it's through your own clairvoyance or your tie to Samson, you know a lot of what's going on right now. Or you can access it, at least. It seems Aidan can see into the past—I mean, were either of you thinking about the discussion he was talking about? If you weren't, he couldn't have got it from run-of-the-mill telepathy."

"*I* don't even know what discussion he was talking about," I told my boyfriend. Uncle Phil shrugged and shook his head no.

"And then we have Ethel Elkins to cover the

future. See? Past, present, and future all accounted for."

I shivered, but I didn't know why.

"While that is interesting, we haven't really *dealt* with your friend Aidan yet, Charlotte," my mother pointed out. "And I think dealing with Aidan might be fairly imperative. The young man is having flashes of retrocognition, and he hasn't even crossed the border of the Magical Midway yet. He is slightly awakened now. It seems like we have no choice but to bring him across and deal with it one way or another."

"The norn will know if it's time," Aidan murmured.

"How do you know what a norn is, Aidan?" I asked him.

"I have seen her in dreams," he whispered, his eyes becoming unfocused as he gazed at the ceiling. "She has visited me in the past to talk about the future, and now it's no longer hidden. I know what I must do. She will know when I must do it."

"What do you have to do?"

Aidan's eyes rolled back as he collapsed into Gunther's arms.

. . .

"Ms. Elkins, we need you and Devana, now, please!" I banged on the door. "Are they ignoring us? Maybe they aren't there. It would be just our luck if they left to go do something right at this moment."

"Charlotte, reach out with your feelings," Gunther said.

"What are you, Obi-Wan Kenobi?"

"Who's that?" Gunther asked, confused.

"Oh my gosh," I sighed.

Closing my eyes, I placed my hand on the door and pictured my senses coming out of the palm of my hand like octopus tentacles. The tendrils of energy stretched out into the room I had created days ago seeking to connect with one of the two isolated women.

I suppose it was less disrespectful than merely kicking down the door.

"Well, that was rude!" Ethel Elkins shouted through the door when my tendril poked her between the eyes. "Just because you can do something doesn't mean you should do something, you know! You could have taken my eye out!"

The door opened slowly, and Devana smiled warmly at me. The huntress witch looked tired, almost as if she had not slept in days. Her beautiful green velvet gown was wrinkled, and the golden sleeves were pushed up above her elbows. "I apologize for not hearing you knock," Devana told me. "We were meditating on an issue and somewhat distracted from this plane."

"Clearly, she was able to get our attention, so don't apologize to her after she poked me in the head!" Ms. Elkins snapped as she shuffled toward the door. "What is it you want, girl? Devana and I have many places to visit and many people to talk to. Nothing's changed out here—"

The norn stopped abruptly and stuck her wrinkled face out. Sniffing the air loudly, she gasped. "He's *here*? When did he get here? Oh, I knew that this was going to be a pain in my wrinkled keister wrangling all these young'uns. Isn't that what *you're* here for?" Ethel asked Devana, poking the huntress witch with her cane. "Why didn't you tell me?"

"Your holiness, you had me visiting other worlds by spirit walk," Devana answered evenly. "I am not so talented that I can split my spirit to work in two planes of reality at once."

"Excuses, excuses. Some help you are," the norn grumbled. She scratched her behind vigorously. "My rear end feels like it's been sitting on boxes of concrete for days. So much lounging around and doing nothing for such a busy time."

"Ms. Elkins, we really need your help," I interrupted the old woman's complaining. "My friend has—"

"Developed powers and you are shocked that you knew him in the human world and he's really descended from a witch, yadda yadda, so on and so forth," Ethel groused. She wildly waved her cane around. The old woman's stick came perilously close to my head. "Yes, yes, I get it. So where is he?"

"Well, he's outside the barrier," I explained. "My mother seems to think that his powers have been partially awakened and I have to say with some of the things he's stating, I agree with—"

"You keep telling me things I already know!" Ethel screeched, shoving her face into mine. "Tell me something I don't know, sweet cheeks!"

"I don't know what you don't know!" I fumed at her. "You've been locked in this room for days and haven't spoken to me! How would I know what you know?"

"Well, then *you're* not exactly where we need you to be, are you?" the old woman sighed with exasperation.

"Ms. Elkins—"

"Bring the reader to me." She pointed her finger at me. "You can handle *that*, can't you?"

I could never quite figure out if Ethel Elkins thought too much of me, or too little.

"Yes, ma'am, I can bring the reader to you," I told her with as much calm as I could muster. "I assume that Aidan is the person you're calling the reader?"

"What have we just been talking about? Were you even in this conversation?" Ms. Elkins screeched and thumped me with her forefinger between my eyes. "The one who knows you without the rings, the one who can read the records of what has been, the one who must fully open the book. Bring him *here*."

I nodded and walked back into the main room. Gunther and Devana followed. I turned and raised my eyebrow at Devana, crossing my arms.

She bowed her head.

"Those who see the future can be arrogant about what they know," Devana said. "Please don't be angry with her holiness. She does want the best for us all, and she *wants* to aid you. Please believe that. When you know all that could come to pass, and all that may come to be, it is difficult to understand why others do not see the paths before them. She doesn't mean any harm or insult."

"I get it," I told her. "It doesn't make her snappy comments any easier to deal with when they're happening. Anyway, why are you coming?"

"The present is a finite amount of information," Devana explained. "Your powers require focus, and what you may know in any moment has completely changed in the next moment. It comes with its own form of control. For those with access to the past, your moment is added to their understanding and all the understandings that have come before. When they are first opened fully to it, it can be…overwhelming."

"Is Aidan going to be hurt? If this is gonna hurt him, I'm *not* bringing him across the barrier," I told her. "I don't care if he has some role in this crazy supernatural drama play, or we need him to save the world. I will *not* hurt my friend."

"It will not be pleasant, but it will not kill him," Devana responded. "Her holiness has seen him on the path, and that image of him has become more solid in the past couple of days as his time of empowerment grows closer. He will survive the crossing, of this I am sure," she said.

"Good," I nodded and turned to make my way to the door.

"I go with you to ensure the rest of us do as well," Devana added.

I stopped, turned and stared at the huntress witch.

Everyone buries the lead.

We walked around the perimeter of the Magical Midway to ensure that Aidan's crossing was made at a place that was the most out of sight from any humans who might arrive at the shelter unexpectedly. Aidan moved as if he'd been drugged. Devana and Gunther hauled him along as best they could, but it was painful to watch my friend in such a state.

I felt responsible.

Intellectually, I understood that Aidan Parker's bloodline inheritance had absolutely nothing to do with me. There were partial paranormals in the human world, and since my home awakened them to this knowledge it was inevitable I would see things like this. It was just part of the gig. If I really thought about it, frankly, it's not a surprise that a part-paranormal would be drawn to me without being aware why.

But this was Aidan.

Even though I knew him for a short period of time in my adult life, we bonded so well. I knew his fears and his hopes. I knew what he had wanted so much for his life. I knew how pragmatic he was, what a skeptic he could be. I never would've guessed this was where his life was headed.

And when we walked him across the barrier, where his life was headed would dramatically change. I knew it.

Fortuna, Mark, and Gunther knew precisely what they were getting into when Roland and I changed them from part-paranormal to full supernatural beings. They embraced the change willingly, even felt that transformation was completing them. They began their new lives sure of who they were meant to be.

Aidan had no idea about any of this. Not only that, I would have to ask him to make a choice. A choice he couldn't possibly fully understand.

"This is good," I said as we came to a stop behind the big top. The vast red and white canvas should shield us from any prying eyes.

"Do we walk him across?" Gunther asked.

"I guess you'll have to," I told him as I searched Aidan's face. "Aidan? I don't know if you'll be able to hear me, but here's the situation. This is a paranormal circus. I'm a witch. So are my parents. I've been told that you descended from witches. As soon as you step across this line that you can't see, your powers will be uncovered completely. I can't tell you what that's gonna feel like."

"Charlotte, it will be…okay, I think," Aidan murmured.

"If you don't want to be what you're about to become, I can undo it," I continued, my voice growing thick with emotion. "But you have to make the change before I can undo it. I'm so sorry, Aidan. I don't think it's going to be pleasant. But I can't do anything about that."

"You knew…about…the waiter because you… saw it in my head," Aidan choked out, his head lolling on his neck as Gunther and Devana continue to support his weight. "I can see…he thought I was cute…you sucked as…a wingman…"

Despite my tears, I laughed.

"I will do better…for you…promise."

I nodded. "I'll do whatever I can to make this easier."

"Nothing about this...will be easy...that's okay."

I nodded again and took four steps through the barrier to the Magical Midway grounds. Gunther and Devana held Aidan across from me just outside of the barrier, but I could see the energy of the Magical Midway coursing through him. It was like the bubble was reaching for him to pull him in.

Maybe it was.

"Pass Aidan to me."

I held out my arms as Gunther and Devana walked Aidan forward and delivered him into my outstretched arms. I was grateful for the super strength that the Magical Midway had bestowed on me, because when Aidan crossed the threshold his muscles convulsed like he had stuck his finger in a light socket. They were so tense I was afraid his bones would snap. It was horrifying to watch, more horrifying to feel as he vibrated against me.

Even with my powers, it was a struggle to hold on to him.

"Mom! Calm him down! Soothe him in whatever way you can! Mom, please!"

The tension in my friend's muscles lessened some, but the choking gurgle that echoed from his open mouth continued relentlessly. His eyes were opened wide, and each pupil bounced independently in different directions.

I could hear the dogs barking from the kennel as if they, too, could sense the power rushing through Aidan's body. I struggled to hold Aidan upright. I didn't want his first experience in the paranormal world to be one of humiliation and writhing in the dirt, but I couldn't support him anymore. Gently laying him down, I shouted for a pillow or blanket.

"It…will be over…soon…" Aidan choked out as I held his head in my lap. "You can tell… Devana…there will be no need to kill me today."

Devana's eyes refused to meet mine when I glanced at her.

"No one's going to kill you, Aidan," I told him as I brushed his dark hair from his eyes. "I'm not sure if you know yet, but I'm the most powerful witch on the planet. I definitely wasn't gonna let anyone kill you."

"You can only…stop what you can see…and you've missed…things…"

"Everyone misses things, Aidan. I did the best I could."

"We have to do…better," he smiled as the tremors in his body slowed. "You have all the pieces that you need, now. I was the last…the piece that you needed to do what you need to do."

"What do I need to do?"

"Right now? Help me up," Aidan sat upright and began brushing the dust off of his expensive designer jeans. "I certainly can't greet my new world looking like this, now, can I?"

I scrambled off the ground and reached out a hand to help Aidan. He clasped it tightly and I pulled him up. Once standing, he held fast and wouldn't release me. I raised my head.

"You don't get to feel guilty for this," my friend told me. He pulled me in closer. "I was always who I was. You *don't* get to feel guilty for this. No matter what happens, no matter what path we take from here, I want you to promise me that you will never feel guilty for this."

"Aidan, come *on*," I told him, rolling my eyes. I tried to pull my hand from his and to avoid making the promise he was trying to extract from me, but he held me firm. Admittedly, I had superpowers, and I could yank my hand out of his hand lickety-split, but I didn't.

"I mean it, Charlotte," Aidan insisted, squeezing my hand.

"Sure, sure, no guilt, whatever," I told him. Finally, he released me from his grip, and I motioned for him to follow me. "We need to get you to Ms. Elkins."

"Yes, I know," he said and began walking.

"How do you know?"

"Because it was decided before this moment, so I know," he told me and shrugged. "It's happening, and so it's done."

"I completely don't get what the heck you're talking about."

"You will."

"I thought you couldn't see the future?"

"I can't, but I know you, Charlotte. There hasn't been a mystery invented in this world or the paranormal one that you can't unravel."

CHAPTER 9

"I HAVE ABSOLUTELY NO IDEA WHAT ALL THIS
hubbub is about or why that guy was shaking, but
I thought *I* was the main focus of the issue here?"
Tiffany complained as we walked into my yurt.

"It's...awfully small, Charlotte," Aidan said,
looking around the small pie-shaped section of
the yurt. It was dark, and dingy, with a cot in one
corner and a camping stove in the other. Toward
the back, a towering stack of boxes marked
clothes served as my closet. At least, that's what
we intended the police to think.

"Follow me," I told Aidan, and I walked
through the stack of boxes.

"Oh wow, so it's like the Harry Potter
platform?"

"Something like that," I told him as I stuck my head out of the top box. "To the human police, they look like regular boxes. You just have to make sure when you're leaving that no humans are in here. Obviously," I stuck my hand through the box and pointed at my face, "this could freak them out a little bit."

"You all should go through," Devana said. "I will stand to watch at the tent door. It will ensure you're not seen entering."

I withdrew deeper into the tent. Uncle Phil, my mom, Aidan, Gunther, and Devana soon followed. Tiffany suddenly appeared out of nowhere in front of my face.

"Why are you not *listening to me?*" she shouted, an icy breeze blowing across my nose. "I'm supposed to be a big deal here! You said you would help me! You don't know who killed me, you don't know how I'm supposed to move on, you don't know *anything*!"

"Now, that's not exactly true, is it?" Aidan asked her. "You haven't exactly been forthcoming with information to the Astleys, have you? If you aren't honest, how are they supposed to help you?"

"I don't *know* you. Do I know you? No, I don't. So that means *you* don't know anything."

"You may not know me, Tiffany, but I *do* know you. At least, I know the actions of your life that solidified your path. The choices you made that led you to this place," he told her sincerely.

"You don't know anything about me," she told him as she crossed her arms. "I just got sent here by the judge, no one here knows anything about my life. I don't know these people. I sure don't know you. So can it."

"The dog that you kidnapped was not some sorority dog," Aidan told her. His eyes grew slightly unfocused and his pupils dilated. "The dog was the service dog of a disabled college student who lived in that sorority, not some mascot. You humiliated an animal that spent his life in service to his master, an animal that was a gift from the girl's brother. A gift to make her difficult life just a little bit better."

"You don't know that. How could you *possibly* know that?" Tiffany gasped as she backed away from Aidan.

"The closer my connection to someone, physical or emotional, the more of their book I can read," Aidan said, his eyes returning to focus. "I have access now to everything that has ever happened in the world—as it was experienced, at least. But I need a spirit as a…bookmark, I guess?

I can go a little way out from that person, but not very far."

"Do you know who killed her?" I asked him.

"I...I don't really see information like that," Aidan responded. His eyes became even more unfocused and he swayed on his feet. After a few moments, he shuddered. "I have to see it through someone, follow known threads. I can see it happening, I can feel his anger, I can hear her screams. But no one right now knows who killed her except for the murderer. So there are not many threads I can follow to discover his identity. If that makes any sense?"

"So the more people that have information and the more connections, the more clear it is to you?"

"Isn't that what he just said?" Ethel Elkins snapped. She shuffled into the great room. "We have been waiting for you, young man. Nice of you to finally show up."

"I wasn't aware, previously, that anyone was waiting on me, ma'am," Aidan told her. "It wasn't until I came close to the Magical Midway that I understood what the dreams meant."

"Some reader you are," she harrumphed.

"With all due respect, I wasn't a reader then,

ma'am. At least not that I knew," Aidan pointed out.

"Now don't you get all sassy with me, young man! Remember, you're just here to give us insight into the past. I'm the one that's in charge of the future." She pointed her bony finger. "Since the future's the only thing we can all still screw up, that means I'm the only one in charge."

"With all due respect again, ma'am, it didn't happen that way the *last* time, and now that I've arrived I don't believe it will be happening this time, either." Aidan tilted his head and smiled at her kindly.

"Last time what?" I asked, confused.

"The last time the hands of fate got involved directly with the human and paranormal world," Aidan told me.

"Now, she's not ready to know about that!"

"Again, with all due respect, ma'am—I am the reader of the past. It's not your choice anymore what Charlotte will know of the past and what she will not. It's mine," Aidan responded firmly.

The two stared at one another. Ethel Elkins mouth worked up and down like a fish trying to gasp for oxygen when it was out of the water. Finally, it snapped shut with a thud, and she nodded once.

"Jeez, Aidan, you've just slipped right into a seat on this crazy little train, haven't you?"

"I guess you could say that." Aidan laughed. "To be fair, my particular skill set in our little endeavor allows me to understand very quickly what's happened, and where we are right now. Ms. Elkins understands the past to an extent, because of her age and what she's lived through—"

"Don't you go talking to people about *my age,* young man! Didn't anyone ever teach you not to talk about a woman's age!"

"Of course, ma'am," Aidan nodded and turned back. "You are the most untouched by what has happened in the past, but that's as it should be, Charlotte. Don't let anyone criticize you for your lack of understanding. You are not beholden to the past," he said. With a quick glance at the old woman, he leaned forward and whispered in my ear.

"...or the future."

Gunther, who had been watching this exchange quietly, suddenly spoke up. "What does that mean, exactly? That she's not beholden to the past or the future?"

Ethel Elkins shot an angry look at Aidan.

"Nothing prophesied *must* come to pass, Mr.

Makepeace," Aidan told him gently. "Nothing dictated by the past *must* be adhered to. Charlotte is, as she was *meant* to be, free to choose. Ms. Elkins and I can help her do that, but ultimately, it is the present and the choice that hold sway over us both."

Ethel Elkins crossed her arms and sighed loudly.

"The past," she sighed again. "Always so pompous and annoying and convinced of its own righteousness."

"But necessary," Aidan smiled.

"I'm working on that," the old woman snapped back.

Devana and Ethel Elkins retired again to the old woman's room with the door closed. My mother returned to check on my father at the main house, and Gunther left with Tiffany to see if they could figure out the best course of action to help her move on.

Aidan and I sat down on the sofa.

"I feel like I should explain everything that's gone on to you," I began once we were alone. "But I suspect you know everything with your new power and all. It certainly *seems* like you're a bit more in control of yourself than you were when you spotted Tiffany. Man, the look on your face…"

"I am quite in control," he nodded. "Much is clear to me now. There's no need to go over things from our human past, and as I got closer to the Magical Midway, I seemed to get closer to the truth of this new reality. What happens now? You said I had a choice to make?"

"Well, we probably need to move the midway over to the Makepeace Circus so Roland and I can make you full-blooded if you're sure that's what you want to do. I take it you're planning on staying in the paranormal world?"

"I am, but if you are talking about turning me into a full witch, there is no need. I *am* a full witch."

I stared at Aidan in shock.

"Wait, what? *How?*"

"Did I ever tell you I was adopted?" Aidan asked. I shook my head no. "No, I guess I wouldn't have. It wasn't something I told a lot of people, especially since I was really struggling with the whole gay thing when we met. It would've been just one more thing I was uncomfortable with, I guess."

"I remember," I told him. "And by the way, the night we went out on a 'date'? I didn't actually peek into the head of the waiter, dude. We had just met that night. So the wingman crack *wasn't* really fair."

"I know, I was really just teasing you," he laughed. "It seemed like an easy way to lighten up what was a really tense moment. I didn't need psychic power to tell you were struggling with it."

"I just remember how hard it was, going from the regular world into this paranormal one," I told him. "I didn't want to do that to you. Or, I guess, it's not exactly that. It's that you clearly were unable to rationally think it through. But I had to do it to you, anyway."

"This is who I've always been, Charlotte. Now that I have this power, I understand that my birth parents knew I was a history reader. We aren't born very often, only in times of great shifting. My mother knew it was likely the Witches' Council would have me killed as soon as they found out about my existence."

"They would have a *baby* killed?" I asked, shocked.

"They would do almost anything to keep their power over other paranormals," he responded. "They have grown corrupt over time, more corrupt and better at making people accept the reasoning of it. I can tell *that* just from reading my own parents' motivations and seeing the threads of your own immediate history."

"So to protect you, your mom gave you up for adoption to someone in the human world?"

"Not to someone," Aidan said. "To someone she *didn't* know. She didn't know who I wound up with. It was a closed adoption, and though she could have worked to discover my whereabouts, she had a psychic block placed within her mind by her own mother so she wouldn't remember any of the information she would have needed to find me."

"Wow. That's crazy. Is your mother still alive?" I asked.

"I don't know," he said. "I can only see before this moment. *You're* the witch in charge of the present. Do *you* think she's alive?"

"Aidan, I never thought my power was all that big a deal. I can just sense something from one person, and only if they're screaming it in their head, or I'm really concentrating. It hasn't gotten any more vast since I became ringmaster, either," I said.

"Your power is much more vast than you give it credit for," Aidan said as his fingers tapped my hand gently. "Your parents have done the same thing that my birth parents did, dissuading you from experiencing your magical side until it was time."

"Wait a minute—are you saying my parents *know* about all this? That's impossible! They've never said *anything*, I've never seen anything in their minds that would give me even an inkling of this!"

"And with a psychic block, that's *entirely* possible. Your folks may not even be aware of what's locked in their minds. What we are would be known at birth, Charlotte. Unless magic hid it."

What Aidan was telling me was stunning, a conspiracy to hide children going back to the beginning of my life and Aidan's life. Yet it didn't fit with what I knew.

"But I didn't get my powers, my major powers until I was the ringmaster. I mean, that's the only reason I'm in this role at all, with this whole paradigm shift thing. It could have just as easily been someone else. It may not even *be* me. It could be Gunther. There are *two* circuses left. We are *both* thirteenth generation circus witches."

Aidan crossed his legs and set down his drink.

"There are some things you don't understand yet about the circus powers," he began.

For the next two hours, Aidan explained the origin of the circus powers, the reason for the circuses, and how the mysterious circus powers were tied to the magic that animated the angry, vicious leadership of Mina World.

"You know all this from your own power to read the past?" I asked Aidan once he was done.

"My power, and I suspect your power as well, works in degrees. If I'm trying to read your history, I can see snippets and flashes and moments of all those you have been connected to. It's like you are the center of the wheel, and as the spokes move away from you into the wider world, I can follow them."

"How far?"

"Ah, *there's* the limitation." He tilted his head. "The further away I go from you, the less information I can access. It's not an unbroken road from point A to point B. It's a bit like a puzzle, really. I only understand as much as I do because you have been at the center of the culmination of the prophecy. Mina World has directly confronted you, and she is part of the other half."

"She's confronted me multiple times, actually," I told him with a sigh.

"Now, keep in mind, I know what I know, but I *don't* know what I can't see. I don't even know if there *is* more. To me, it seems like a complete story, but because of how this works, there may be things I'm not aware of. People you haven't come into contact with yet, or who are too far from you for me to get a clear picture of them. Aspects that haven't been set into motion yet."

"People's histories that you can't read," I said.

"Precisely," he nodded.

"I can't believe we're sitting here and talking about this." I got up to put the empty glasses in the sink. "I mean, it seems bizarre that you're here *at all*, much less calmly explaining my own paranormal history to me. I swear, my life just gets weirder and weirder."

"I think if I didn't have the power that I do, I'd probably be dealing with this a lot worse," he smiled. "I'm supposed to be a help to you, a reference, and I guess sometimes a guide. I wouldn't be a very good one if I were lying on the floor babbling incoherently because I'm freaking out over the fact that ghosts exist."

"Or witches," I added.

"Or kelpies, magical circuses, the Witches' Council—I mean, take your pick. This would be a lot to take in. Luckily, apparently, I already did. I just didn't realize it was locked within me. Or remember, I guess…I don't know, you know what I mean."

I nodded and walked back toward Aidan, who was still sitting on the couch.

"I know I haven't really said this yet, but I'm thrilled you're here."

"Me, too, Charlotte," he told me quietly. "I really missed you. And honestly? I wasn't doing all that well with my human life, truth be told."

"You're dating a hot cop. That's not doing too bad," I pointed out.

Aidan gestured for me to sit down on the couch. His calm and confident expression wavered, and the slight smile he had worn since he got up off the ground turned into a frown. He sighed.

"We *barely* have a relationship, really. I mean, we do? But there's just no depth to it. Kyle is… Kyle is cute, and he can be nice. We get along for the most part, but we do a lot of stuff that just… doesn't involve communicating at all."

"Oh my," I breathed.

"Not like that!" Aidan protested. "I mean, going to see plays or movies where we don't really need to talk about anything. Just experience something sitting side-by-side, then he drops me off at home, gives me a kiss on the cheek, and it's over. It's over a month that we've been dating, and I still don't know that much about him. We don't talk, and so it all goes nowhere."

"How about your job? How's that going? It must be horrible working with Bobby after everything that happened."

"I left it after...well, you know," Aidan said. "Bobby was such a jerk after Tabitha dumped him. He blamed me. It never occurred to him at all that it was his reaction to my being gay that caused Tabitha to leave him."

"No, it wouldn't occur to him, would it?" I had never liked Bobby. Aidan coming out just demonstrated *why* I never liked Bobby.

"I left the bank within a couple of weeks. It just became impossible for the two of us to work together. Bobby couldn't manage to be polite, he blamed me for everything, and I just didn't want to deal with making a complaint to the bank about how he was treating me. It was easier just to go."

"So where you working now?"

"The Police Department, actually," Aidan said. "I do forensic accounting. If someone's embezzling, committing fraud, I use my quite boring but useful accounting skills to figure out where the crime is."

"That sounds more exciting than investment banking."

"It is. I like puzzles, so it was a perfect fit for me," he nodded. "I met Kyle when he and I were working on a case. We seem to get along really well, and he was really interested in what I was doing, which was cool. What I do is boring, even when it's exciting," Aidan laughed.

"If you enjoy it, it doesn't matter if it's boring. Won't be boring to you."

"Anyway, that's pretty much been my life," Aidan said. "Won't be all that much to leave, I guess. One mostly failed relationship, and a job where the major player that I should be able to convict I'll never be able to because no prosecutor or judge will allow the evidence in."

"Who's that?"

"Anthony Drake," Aidan responded with more of an edge to his voice than I'd ever heard before from him. "I swear, that guy has more law enforcement in his pocket. He is like Teflon. Nothing sticks to him."

"You worked on a case where he was the subject?"

"No, I've worked on cases where people were kicking back to him. For some reason, once I trace the money up the chain and hit Anthony Drake or one of his shell companies, every investigation gets shut down within twenty-four hours. It's the most frustrating thing about my job. I won't be sorry to walk away."

"Wow," I said. "I guess it was job security, at least."

"Not the kind I wanted. I think I was getting ready to quit even before this happened. There's only so many times I could deal with hitting that wall. I realized a couple of weeks ago I was never going to be able to get him. Even if I got him, no one would've used the evidence to bring Drake and his cronies up on charges—much less convict them of anything. I was just spinning my wheels."

"I'm so sorry, Aidan. That must've been really frustrating."

"It was. I'm excited to get on with all of this," he said as he waved his arms. "You going to give me a job? I could do the books for the circus."

"I don't know that we have books..." I told him slowly.

"Do you make money?"

"Well, yeah, I guess," I responded.

"Then you have to have books."

"Talk to Uncle Phil about it. He's probably been doing them. Are you gonna tell Kyle you're joining the circus?"

"Oh wow, I am, aren't I?" Aidan exploded with laughter. "I'm running away to join the circus. How funny is that? There's something to mark off my bucket list. Aidan Parker running away to join the *circus*."

"I'm glad it's making you so happy," I responded. "I hope you're still happy after living in a yurt for a week. I have a futon in my room, you can bunk with me until we figure out where you're going to stay more permanently."

"I don't think it's going to make Ethel Elkins happy."

"I think you're probably right about that."

"Mind if we interrupt?" Gunther asked as he stuck his head in the great room.

"Hey, we were just chatting. What's up?"

"The reason Tiffany Drake was here was a little more complicated than she present—"

"They don't need to know about all this! You

just stop!" Tiffany screeched from somewhere behind him.

Gunther winced, but continued.

"...than she presented to us. Your dad and I discovered some information on the lookup screen. Can we come in?"

"Do you have to bring Tiffany?"

"I heard that!"

CHAPTER 10

GUNTHER LOOKED LIKE HIS ENERGY HAD BEEN drained dry by the demanding, argumentative young ghost. He sat down into a wingback chair next to us with a sigh.

"Forgive me for intruding, but I can see in your past that you don't always look like this," Aidan told Gunther. "Are you all right?"

"Tiffany seems to have an unlimited amount of energy as a ghost," Gunther told him. "She also has an unlimited amount of questions, an unlimited amount of demands, and an unlimited amount of complaints."

"Look, circus boy, I don't want to be here any longer than I have to. The best way for you to get me out of here is to help me. You're looking in all the wrong places!"

"What's that all about?" I asked him.

"Your father typed on the box that comes up with the human information?"

"A computer? You mean the Internet?" I asked Gunther slowly as Aidan chuckled. Gunther's eyes jumped over to my friend with a frown.

"I'm unfamiliar with the proper terms in the human world," Gunther responded somewhat defensively.

"No problem, Gunther. I didn't mean anything by it, sorry if the way I said that came off as..."

"Condescending?" he asked.

Aidan's grin faded as he looked back and forth between Gunther and me.

"Sorry, I'll try not to do that. You're right, you haven't had any experience with this. Anyway, what did you guys find on your search?"

"The sorority house has a fundraiser once a year. The one that Tiffany kidnapped the dog from?"

"You can't *kidnap* a dog! It's not a *person*. A dog is *property*. At best, I *stole* a worthless piece of property. It was just a mutt, not some expensive show dog."

The three of us stared at the heartless girl with undisguised disgust. Though the animals that inhabited both the circuses were mostly shapeshifters, knowing those shapeshifters and their animal natures had given Gunther insight into the personalities and feelings of the animals that inhabited the human world. I grew up in an animal shelter rescuing abandoned creatures from irresponsible humans. Aidan was just an animal lover. All three of us were repulsed by her statement.

Tiffany, however, was oblivious to our reaction.

"I'm just going to ignore anything she interjects so I can get through this without getting angry." Gunther's face tensed. "The sorority house's major donor is Anthony Drake. We came across an invitation for a fundraising dinner that honored him for all his contributions."

"Honored him *personally*?"

"Well, his company," Gunther said.

"And I told this idiot that couldn't have possibly happened." Tiffany set herself on the coffee table in the center of the three of us. "My father would never have given money or supported a rival sorority. Especially not *that* sorority!"

"What's wrong with that sorority?" I asked her.

"Alpha Omicron Kappa. I mean, is that not the *stupidest* name you ever heard for a sorority?"

"It's three Greek letters which are pretty usual, isn't it?"

"I can't believe I have to explain it to you. Yes, it's three Greek letters. A O K? They were the first sorority on campus to accept disabled people and stupid people and…"

"Wait, do you mean people with developmental and physical disabilities?" Aidan asked.

"Isn't that what I *just* said? The a-okays are slow, and always messing up the games, and the library was all messed up because of a stupid ramp…"

"Okay, wait a minute, wait a minute…You *stole a dog* from a sorority whose members include people with developmental and physical disabilities who have managed to go to college? Do I have this right?"

"You have it right," Gunther sighed.

"What? What's the problem?" Tiffany asked, crossing her arms.

"Oh no," I whispered, staring at Aidan. He stared back and said nothing. What he said when he was in his hazy trance came back to me like a slap upside my head.

"Oh no, what?" Tiffany asked.

"When you kidnapped the dog, was it wearing anything?"

"Like a sweater?"

"Like anything. A collar, a placard, anything."

"It had some stupid like harness jacket thing, like it was going to go swimming or something."

"Oh, you have *got* to be kidding me," I said as I stared at her, horrified. "You stole a disabled person's *service dog*? What is *wrong* with you?"

"It was just a stupid dog!"

"I don't understand what this means. What's a service dog?" Gunther asked.

"In the human world," Aidan said, once he realized I was too shocked and horrified to speak, "dogs can be trained to help human beings who are born with or develop various health problems. Sometimes those health problems prevent them from being able to do everything in life that they want to do independently. The dog helps them, supports them, ensures that even with a disability that human can live a full life."

"What a remarkable bond they must develop

with one another," Gunther said appreciatively. Then his face froze as he realized the full magnitude of what Tiffany had done. He turned and stared at her, disgust spreading across his face again. "I agree with Charlotte. You were a *horrible* human being. Why would you *do* such a thing?"

"I wasn't thinking about it! It was a joke!" she shouted. Gunther continued to stare at her. "Stop looking at me like that!"

"I honestly can't believe someone didn't kill you sooner," Gunther mumbled.

"Don't you start getting judgmental on me, circus boy," Tiffany snapped. She jumped to her transparent feet and placed her sparkly fists on her hips. "You all promised to help me. Doesn't matter what I did. I can't undo it. There's nothing to be done about it *now*."

"That *is* a shame," I told her. "It's a shame that some things can't be undone. Because if this could, I would undo it in a heartbeat."

"I do have to wonder why you are so eager to move on from here," Aidan asked.

"Because it's dirty and boring and I don't like any of you people!"

"If *I* were you," Aidan responded slowly. "I would be seriously concerned about just what eternity waited for me. Considering who you were in life and all."

"What do you mean?" Tiffany asked him suspiciously.

"Just that the universe tends to prefer balance in all things. When things are out of balance, people and paranormals both can suffer. I can say without question, Ms. Drake, that you lived your life quite out of balance."

"Oh my God. Getting whacked in the head with a paver stone wasn't enough suffering? *Really?*"

"The act of death? You don't even recall it, do you?"

"N-no..."

"When the universe comes to balance the scales, Ms. Drake? I have a feeling you will be acutely aware of it. As aware as the girl is of her pain over her lost companion, as aware as the dog was of its pain over abandoning his companion due to *your* actions. The past comes for us *all*, Ms. Drake. Eventually."

I shivered at Aidan's words and Gunther looked pale.

Tiffany Drake, however, rolled her eyes and disappeared from the great room.

"Aidan?" I said quietly.

"Yes?"

"You're kinda super creepy now. Just a little."

"Sorry about that."

"No problem. I'm sure I'll get used to it."

"I don't know about that," Gunther exhaled.

"Well, I can certainly take a stab in the dark and guess why someone would want to kill her," I told Aidan and Gunther. "I think we have to go over to the a-okays sorority house. It sounds to me like that's where our most likely suspect is."

"Don't you think the police are probably there?" Gunther asked.

"Aidan, you are the police. What you think?"

Aidan shook his head no. "Kyle is assuming that Tiffany was killed because of something her father did. I've seen this before. He's a good detective, but he's got a blind spot when it comes to Anthony Drake. I don't think it would occur to him that anyone would kill a nineteen-year-old girl because of something she did."

"Do people often kill over dogs in your world?" Gunther asked.

"No. Probably more often than we like to think, but not in general, no," I told him. Looking at my watch, I realized it was already mid-afternoon. That didn't leave me a lot of time to go do anything and then get back before sundown.

"How far is the sorority house, do you think?" I asked Aidan.

"In this traffic? At least forty-five minutes."

"That means it would take an hour and a half just to get there and back," I told him. "If we leave now, I don't think I'll be able to get back onto the grounds of the Magical Midway until tomorrow morning."

"Why is that?"

"Whatever side of the barrier she's on as the sun sets or rises, that's the side that she'll be on for the entire night or day."

"Right, of course," Aidan nodded as if information within his mind was suddenly clarified. "It is unlikely that the Magical Midway would face any threat from the Witches' Council during this time—if that's a primary concern. With the police attention, they wouldn't dare make a move."

"That's a good point," I told Gunther. "Even if I can't get back on the fairgrounds themselves, we can just sleep in the main house. My parents have plenty of extra room."

It will be fine. Just go.

Samson?

The sooner you solve this, the sooner we leave, and the sooner I can stop this. Do whatever you must do. I will handle it here. Just go.

"Samson says he can handle protecting the Magical Midway if I can't get back, which is likely."

"I have my car, so I'll be happy to drive. I can also swing by my apartment and get clothing and items that I'll need when we leave," Aidan volunteered.

"When we leave?" Gunther asked, confused.

"Yes, I'll be coming with you when the Magical Midway moves on to its next destination," Aidan told him. "I could explain all the reasons for that, prophecy this and future that and knowing the past blah blah blah, but in reality, I'm kind of excited for reasons apart from any magical ones."

"You seem to have adjusted awfully quickly to your new life," Gunther observed. His words were tinged with just a shade of suspicion.

"It's a side effect of my magical ability," Aidan told him and smiled. "When my powers were fully awakened, I had access to my own past in a way that I never had before. Self-awareness came more quickly than I ever would've expected. I feel a little silly struggling all those years with who I am. Now it all seems so clear."

"That must be nice," Gunther said wryly.

"You're closer than you think," Aidan responded kindly. "You're struggling far too much with…"

Aidan stopped short and glanced at me.

"My apologies, Gunther, I didn't mean to offer advice when it wasn't asked for, and I shouldn't have said anything in front of another without your permission. Please know that I am here for all of you, not just Charlotte. I would be happy to talk to you about your story whenever you wish."

"Maybe let's leave the self-examination until after we solve Tiffany's murder," Gunther told him. "I, for one, would really love for that girl to move on. I've met unpleasant creatures in my lifetime, but she really takes the cake."

"Is there cake? Oh, awesome, I want some cake!" Bob Larry called excitedly as he walked into the yurt. "I timed this just right! Oh, hey! Who are *you*, now?"

My Roman hippie guard casually strolled in, twirling his spear as if it were a baton. The handsome, goofy lares eyed Aidan with interest as he waited to be introduced.

"Bob, this is my friend Aidan, and he's going

to be staying with us from now on," I told him. "Aidan, this is Bob. He's one of five lares guards that we have at the Magical Midway. They're Roman—"

"I can read his story, Charlotte," Aidan said without taking his eyes off Bob. "No need to explain to me. What an incredibly unique story it is…"

"That's me, Aidan, super unique! All the strength and fierceness of a Roman warrior wrapped in the cuddly exterior of an impish kitten," Bob said proudly. "I can promise you that you'll never meet another lar like *me*."

"No, I wouldn't think so," Aidan answered.

My eyes traveled back and forth between Aidan and Bob as the two men stared at one another, and my intuition lit up like a Christmas tree. Wait, was Bob *gay*? I thought back to the conversations we had, and I could never recall him saying he liked anyone romantically, one way or another. Not a man, not a woman, not even a species.

I shrugged. With Aidan's new power, he was more than capable of figuring out whether Bob was or wasn't someone he should be attracted to. I looked over at Gunther. He looked back at me, amused.

"Anyway, what did you need, Bob?"

"Anya wanted me to let you know that she and Avalon are handling the deer herd, and though they're doing okay, they are getting a bit nervous. Fortuna and Fiona have gone over there to help her, since Fortuna can sense how fearful they are, and Fiona…well, she really just likes to be in the middle of things, doesn't she?"

I chuckled.

"Everything else is kind of steady as she goes," Bob said with a haphazard bow. "Anything else I can do for you, Charlotte, you just let me know. Unless it has to do with that old woman in there," Bob whispered. He jutted his chin in Ethel Elkins' general direction. "That old lady *scares* me."

"I heard that!" a screech exploded from behind the closed door.

"See? That *ain't* normal," Bob said, shaking his head.

"Just to let you know, Bob, Gunther and I are going to be leaving the grounds. There's a good chance we won't be back by sundown, but Samson's assured me that everything will be fine overnight. We'll sleep up at the main house and be back in the morning."

"You going to leave handsome down here with me to keep me company?" Bob smiled mischievously at Aidan and wiggled his eyebrows. Aidan laughed and struggled not to blush.

"Handsome is coming with us," I told him. "He's got a car, and we need to pick up some things for him so he can move in."

"So, tell me about Bob." Aidan's eyes scanned the empty rural highway. The blue sedan traveled right at the speed limit. I sat in the passenger side and Gunther looked out at the Texas prairie from the backseat. I chuckled partially at his question and partially at his conservative car driving just within the rules. "Have you known him long?"

"Since I was a girl and first came to the Magical Midway," I answered fiddling with the radio. "Why are you asking me about Bob, Aidan? Can't you, like, read his whole story and tell everything about him?"

"Not precisely," he said. We came upon a slow tractor, driving ten miles an hour to get from one field to another. Flipping on his blinker, even though there wasn't a car behind us for miles, Aidan slid us into the passing lane. "I can see things that happened, images and information, but it's very dry. Almost academic. It doesn't tell me who he *is*, not really."

"It seemed to tell you who Ethel Elkins was," Gunther observed. "I mean, whatever you saw in your head certainly seem to inform what you told her. It seemed personal to me."

"That was a little different," Aidan told him while he glanced in the rearview mirror. "Ethel Elkins is in charge of the future from her perspective, and I hold the key to understanding the past. To some extent, these roles are always tugging on one another, trying to pull the balance right."

"Interesting," Gunther said, though it didn't sound like he thought it was interesting.

"So why do you want to know about Bob, Aidan?" I teased.

"I was just curious, that's all," he replied as nonchalantly as he could. "Charlotte, have you talked to Tabitha since you left?"

"Wouldn't you know?" I asked him, confused.

"It doesn't *seem* like you have, but frankly, I'm not entirely sure that I can see absolutely everything, especially if something happens that didn't really have a consequence. So let's just assume that if I'm asking a question, you don't have to counter with asking whether I should know or not."

"Well, what it seems like is what it is. I wanted to give her some space, and then I left. Actually, I think I told you that already."

Aidan's face tense for a moment and then he nodded. "This is harder than I thought," he said in a voice so low I wasn't sure if he was talking to me or talking to himself.

"What's wrong?"

"It's just a lot of information, and I'm starting to have trouble separating what I know because I *experienced* it, and what I know because of the psychic access I have to people's timelines. The memories that are my own are starting to…just mix in with everything else."

"Are you going to be okay?" Gunther asked, concerned. "Should we pull over and have Charlotte drive?"

"I don't *think* so," Aidan answered after a few moments. "I don't think I'll lose skills that I've learned. At least, at the moment I don't think I will. I'm fine to drive."

"Isn't that it?" I pointed to the exit that would head toward the college. Sorority Circle was located a few blocks away from the college. It was a small college, outside of Austin proper, and from what I remembered there were only five sororities on the campus. I explained to Gunther how each house lined a cul-de-sac at the end of fraternity row.

"So there are these five houses, like five competing covens, and they all live on the same circled street next to one another?"

"Wait, we have covens?"

"Of course we do," Gunther told me. "Well, we are circus people, so *we* don't. But there are dozens of covens in Impy."

"What about the other towns?"

"Covens are only allowed in Impy, and only after being chartered by the Witches' Council."

"Of course. Why did I even ask? In any case, to answer your previous question, yes, the sororities all live next to each other. They're not really supposed to be rivals, though. I mean, they are, but it's supposed to be friendly."

"Someone kidnapped and killed a dog," Gunther murmured as civilization moved past the window. "That doesn't sound like a friendly rivalry to me."

"The dog's death was not intentional," Aidan said without looking away from the traffic. "I do agree that Ms. Drake's personality has been warped by her father's...unique view of morality.

She kidnapped the dog and displayed it outside in the outfit of her own sorority's mascot."

"Which was?"

"An owl," he said. "The costume, however, was not really a costume. It was a rubber encasement. The dog suffocated within an hour."

"How do you know that the dog's death wasn't intentional?"

"I have the memory of the discussion about pulling the prank," Aidan said. "She did not perform this prank alone, but she did take the fall for the others that were involved."

"Could one of them have killed her?"

"She was kicked out of the college. I saw that on the court papers," I told Gunther as our eyes met in the mirror. "How many other people were involved?"

"Two other sorority sisters that I saw," Aidan said.

"Would you recognize them if you saw them?"

"Yes, definitely."

"So we need to visit both sorority houses," I said.

"And we now have two houses full of suspects," Gunther said.

"Two houses full of sorority girls," Aidan pointed out. He pulled the car into the sorority house cul-de-sac. Gazing at the old houses, he turned back and sighed. "If those girls are *anything* like Tiffany Drake, this may take us a while."

If those girls are anything like Tiffany Drake, any of them could've killed her.

CHAPTER 11

We climbed the ramp in front of the Alpha Omicron Kappa house slowly. The slope was a gentle, zigzagging pattern and clearly designed more for the comfort of those pushing a wheelchair than those who could walk up. There were no stairs to bypass the three sloping levels that led to the house's front door.

"Don't climb over that," I told Aidan as he threw his leg over one of the handrails.

"Why not?" he asked me, confused.

"I don't know. It just doesn't seem right somehow," I told him, biting my lower lip. "I mean, they could've made stairs. They didn't. So just go up the ramp the way they laid it out."

"Um, okay, Charlotte." Aidan lowered his leg. "I was just trying to save a couple of seconds."

"I get it," I nodded.

I wasn't sure why Aidan sprinting over the barriers didn't sit right with me. Maybe it was something about the fact that many girls who lived in this house couldn't, and so jumping over the handrails seem disrespectful somehow. It felt impatient. Entitled, even.

Tiffany Drake's attitude was getting to me.

When we reached the top, I rang the doorbell, and a cheerful chime echoed from behind the door.

"Hello? Can I help you?" someone called from within the house.

"Hi, we were hoping to talk to someone about the animal abuse that took place a couple of months ago? Is the person that owned the dog in?"

The door opened, and as it slowly widened, a dark-haired girl in a wheelchair stared out at us from behind black-rimmed glasses. "Who are you?" she asked suspiciously.

"I work for the police department, ma'am," Aidan jumped in, pulling out a badge that may or may not have been real, for all I knew. "A couple of days ago, a Tiffany Drake was murdered. We just wanted to swing around and ask a few questions, just in case what happened to her had anything to do with what happened to the dog."

"The dog's name was Destiny," the girl said quietly. Tears filled her eyes. "And she wasn't *the* dog. She was *my* dog."

"I'm so terribly sorry," I told her. The girl's wave of grief and pain and loss flowed over me. I felt guilty for provoking it. "The loss of a pet is always excruciating, and this must've been much worse than that for you."

"Because the person that was supposed to watch out for me is the one that killed her?" the girl snapped.

"Supposed to watch out for you?" I asked. The young woman stared directly back at me for a long time. Then she sighed and rolled backward making room for us.

"Why don't you just come in? It doesn't seem like you really know much about what happened here. That doesn't really surprise me." The girl wheeled backward to allow us room to come in. "Tiffany always managed to get out of everything and hide the truth from everyone. Not sure why this would be any different."

"Melissa, are you okay?" a beautiful blonde girl asked as she came down the stairs.

"Yeah, I'm fine. These folks want to talk about what happened with Destiny. Apparently, someone killed Tiffany a couple of days ago," Melissa told her, wheeling into the central sitting area off the hallway. The young woman's words brought her friend to a stop and her jaw dropped.

"Wow, are you kidding? She's *dead*? Someone actually *killed* her?" The blonde made a quick sign of the cross.

"Yep. Not kidding. At least I'm not unless they are." Melissa gestured to us.

"No, it's been all over the news," I told her. "I'm surprised you didn't already know."

"We're both taking summer classes," Melissa responded and shrugged. "We're lucky we remember to eat, honestly."

No one so far seemed remotely broken up about the fact that a young woman close to their age had been murdered. No one asked why; neither of these girls looked sad at all. There wasn't even a rampant set of rumors or gossip about her death. For a moment I felt a twinge of sympathy for Tiffany, so disliked that no one seemed to care too much she was dead.

Tiffany killed this girl's dog, Gunther thought. *I don't know that I'd be very broken up about it, either, if I were her.*

He had a point.

"Let me know if you need anything, okay?" The blonde girl said.

"No problem, I'm good," Melissa told her as we all sat down.

"Is she, um..." Gunther's voice trailed off as he watched the able-bodied blonde girl walk on her own power out of the room. I winced as Melissa's eyes narrowed. Everyone realized what he was about to say all at the same moment.

The same moment he realized it was probably not a question he should be asking.

"Where is she *broken*, you mean? You must've met Tiffany before she died," Melissa told Gunther with an edge to her voice. "Our sorority is full of idiots, rejects, and retards, right? I'm sure that's what you were told."

"I don't think that's what he meant," Aidan interjected. "We had been told, however, that this was a sorority for those with disabilities of all types. One of the first sororities of its kind, in fact."

"Yeah, no, that's not exactly it," Melissa said. "This is a sorority like *any* other sorority. You have to be of good moral character to join, you have to be smart, you have to get good grades. All of the normal sorority stuff. The only difference is that our sorority doesn't *exclude* people *just* because they're disabled. So there are able-bodied people here, and there are disabled people here. And frankly, a lot of the time you won't be able to tell who is who."

"That still goes on? The exclusion, I mean," I asked her. "Isn't that against the law somehow?"

"Officially? Of *course* it doesn't go on," Melissa said as she rolled her eyes. "Lawsuits and all, right? Unofficially? Pledge week was *designed* to weed out the *undesirables*. It's effortless to make sure that someone is unable to complete the challenges of pledge week because they're disabled. If that's what you want to do, anyway. And most sororities and fraternities do."

"I'm sincerely sorry if I offended with my almost-question," Gunther told her. "I realized as soon as my mouth started moving that it was an insulting thing to say."

"Apology accepted," she nodded.

Gunther looked relieved. My boyfriend really was considerate , but unfamiliar with navigating this human terrain. Every time I brought him near my human life or even talked about it, it's like I would knock him off his game. All this was a lot to handle, and I never even prepared him for human etiquette.

Well, not much.

"So, what is it you think we're unclear on? I really would like to know the story," I told Melissa. "Even if it doesn't help us figure out who might've killed Tiffany, my parents run the animal shelter that she volunteered at. She was a...strange girl. I guess I'm kind of curious how she got that way."

"I didn't know her that well. Actually, I didn't really know her at all," Melissa said. "But I can sure tell you how she got that way."

"From everything I heard, before she met her father she wasn't that bad," Melissa told us as we sat around the light-colored living room of the AOK house. "I mean, she was under ten, so I guess there's not really that much you can do before you're ten years old and all. There was a girl in my biology class that knew her when she was growing up, though. Carla said they used to be friends, because Tiffany *used* to be nice."

"And then she met her father?"

"Yeah, I'm not even really clear how that happened," Melissa nodded. "I don't know if her mom needed money for something. I heard something about her mom being, like, really poor and applying for services? Apparently in Texas when you apply for services you, like, have to go after the dad if he's not paying child support."

"If you need to apply for welfare or Medicaid in the state, the mother would've had to document that she had attempted to get child support for her child," Aidan said. "The state essentially goes to get it for her to offset what they spend to help."

"I bet that went over with Anthony Drake *really* well," I told him.

"Yeah, the rumors are he didn't know about her until the state showed up and started threatening him and stuff, which, yeah, I guess he wasn't too happy about," Melissa said with a wince.

"Are you all right?" Gunther leaned forward.

"Yeah, I get these weird phantom pains in my legs," she said as she exhaled. "I was in a car accident when I was really young, and I was paralyzed from the waist down. So, I technically shouldn't feel anything. Heck, if you poke me with a pin, I won't even notice it. But sometimes, for no reason, my legs hurt. It's the *weirdest* thing."

We nodded, unsure of what to say.

"Though not the weirdest thing, really. One of

my sorority sisters actually has her leg amputated, and it hurts, too. Maybe *that's* the weirdest thing. Anyway, so Tiffany's Dad kinda swooped in? I don't think her mom was really happy."

"I thought her mother was hit by a car when she was ten years old?" I asked Melissa.

"Yeah, she was, but the way *I* heard it, that car hit her *after* Anthony Drake showed up, and after she and Anthony Drake got into *lots* of fights about Tiffany and him being in her life," Melissa said. "The rumor was that mom wanted to keep Tiffany as far away from Anthony Drake as possible. Anthony Drake did not agree…if you get my drift."

Aidan, Gunther, and I instantly looked at one another. I didn't even have to use my power to know what they were thinking. It was the same thought I had.

"Carla used to go over to her house and play all the time, and then one day Tiffany's mom died, and Tiffany just disappeared from the apartment they had been living in. Like, gone. Carla looked through the window, and all the furniture was still there, Tiffany's toys on the floor. Even pictures on the wall. But she never came back to the neighborhood."

"So Carla actually saw Anthony Drake around Tiffany while Tiffany's mother was alive? You're *absolutely* sure that's what she said?"

"Yep," she nodded. "She lives in the dorms right down the street. I can call her and ask her to come over if you want."

I thought about it and then shook my head no. "This is really interesting, but I'm not sure that what happened to her when she was ten really has anything to do with her being murdered a few months short of turning twenty."

"Maybe," Melissa said sounding unconvinced. "What happened to her after her mom died, though, probably does. That's when I started to know about her."

"How so?"

"My brother works for Anthony Drake," she shrugged. "He's not particularly *proud* of it or anything. I mean, no one that works for Drake really is, you know? But there are only a few places you can work out here and make a lot of money, and working for Anthony Drake is one of those places."

"Did your family have money issues?" Aidan asked. He held up his hand as if to apologize for asking the question. "I don't mean to pry, but frankly, you seem like a nice girl, and I find it hard to believe that anyone would work for Anthony Drake if there weren't some kind of pressure where they needed a good amount of cash."

"Well, yeah, of course there was," she laughed and waved her hands up and down her wheelchair-bound body. "My parents were killed in the car accident, and it was just me and my brother left. The drunk driver that hit the car didn't have insurance, and he didn't own anything, my parents hardly had any life insurance, so...I mean, yeah, things were kind of desperate. My brother was barely an adult, and suddenly he had to take care of his young, paraplegic sister."

"That must've been terribly hard for him," Aidan told her.

"Sure. My recovery was expensive, and then just buying things so I could live once I recovered...that was expensive, too. I don't really blame Micah for going to work for that jerk. I don't think he knew what else to do, and he didn't want to move."

"Why not?" I asked.

"We had lost so much," she said with a catch in her throat. "We lost our parents, I lost the use of my legs. My parents didn't talk to their families, so we didn't really have anybody other than each other and our life here. He didn't want us to lose our home or for me to lose all my friends. So he did what he had to do to maintain it."

"Doesn't the government take care of its people when they're sick?" Gunther asked, confused.

Aidan, Melissa, and I stared at Gunther, unsure of what to say. I turned back to Melissa and smiled.

"He's Canadian," I told her. She made a sound of comprehension and smiled at him.

Our government does not take care of the sick, I thought quickly to Gunther. *It's a service, so to speak, that you must have the money to pay for.*

But what if you don't?

Then you don't. If it's an emergency, you can have your life saved, but ongoing care? You have to find a way to pay for it, or for someone to pay for it for you. Some people just go without treatment, medicine, healing, because they can't pay for it.

Gunther's face froze in shock, then shifted to disgust.

Your world is not superior in all things, Charlotte.

No, I suppose nobody has it perfect, yet.

Gunther's fingers moved almost imperceptibly in a pattern as his hand lay on his lap. I felt a small rush of magical energy blow through the room. Gunther smiled at me as I caught his eye.

What did you do?

He didn't answer. He just winked.

Aidan cleared his throat.

"Sorry, I was just thinking," I told Melissa. "So your brother, what was his name?"

"Micah."

"So did you meet Tiffany through Micah?"

"No," Melissa said as she shook her head. "He really tried to keep me away from that whole scene, you know? Like, even when I was a girl, Micah tried to hide all of it from me. I guess he didn't want me to realize that he was working for a gangster. But he did say she would check in with me here and watch out for me," Melissa said as she made a face. "Fat good that did. He'd tell me stories about Anthony Drake's family that would make me wonder why he even mentioned me to her at all."

"What kind of stories?" Gunther asked.

Before she could continue, there was a knock at the door. Melissa grabbed a remote control and wheeled herself toward the hallway. She asked who it was as she approached.

"Detective Kyle Roberts," came the answer.

Uh oh.

"I could arrest all three of you right now!" Kyle snapped. He shook his finger at us while we stood on the front porch of the Alpha Omicron Kappa house. Though he was upset with all of us for coming here and talking to Melissa, the preponderance of his finger waving seemed flung in Aidan's direction.

"No, you *really* couldn't," Aidan responded calmly. "We didn't tell anyone to do anything, we just came to ask questions because we were curious. I'm sure if you go back in and have a conversation with Melissa, she'll be happy to let you know that we have not *interfered* with anything."

"This case is complicated enough as it is without having the three of you poking around," Kyle told Aidan, crossing his arms. "I've got the chief breathing down my neck telling me to just drop it, and I've got you running around with someone I knew from high school and...who are you, exactly?"

"I'm Charlotte's boyfriend," Gunther said nodding in my direction.

"Are you in the habit of letting your girlfriend run around in the middle of murder investigations?" Detective Roberts asked him.

"Aren't you dating Aidan? I suppose I could ask you the same question. At least, I *would* ask you the same question if it wasn't so insulting to Aidan."

"What are you talking about?" Kyle snapped again.

"Charlotte and I are in a *relationship*. She's not some pet I keep on a leash," Gunther snapped back at him. "The fact that you even *implied* otherwise is offensive."

Wow. Go Gunther.

"I would suggest that we take this animated discussion further down the ramp," Aidan said quietly. "We are beginning to attract eyes that we would probably prefer not to attract. No doubt ears will follow, and we're not making a terribly good impression of the local police department's professionalism."

"You care about that *now*, do you?" Detective Roberts said as he lowered his voice and quickly scanned the faces looking out of various windows around the cul-de-sac.

"Are you implying I can't professionally ask questions, honey?" Aidan asked Kyle sarcastically.

"I have a badge the same as you. I may not be a detective, but I *am* an investigator."

"You're an *accountant*," Kyle argued.

"You're insulting," Aidan retorted with an edge, even as he placed a hand on Kyle's shoulder supportively. "I get that you're having a bad day, but you don't need to treat us like this. We're all looking for the truth. And frankly, Kyle, you look like you could use the help. Is it just you here?"

Kyle glared angrily at Aiden. He turned on his heel, and walked down the ramp, glancing back once to ensure we were following him.

Once in the street, we stood in a circle beside his police SUV, using the vehicle to block us from the view of three of the sorority houses.

"You're right," Kyle told Aidan. "I've had my *entire* team gutted in a matter of hours. Captain Johansson made some crack about how some college girl being killed in an animal shelter wasn't worth the number of man-hours we were paying, and he reassigned everyone. Everyone but me."

"Everyone knows Johansson's in Drake's pocket," Aidan pointed out. "You had to have expected that he would pull something like that as soon as he heard."

"I *never* expect it," Kyle told him. "I should,

though. It keeps happening." Detective Roberts rubbed his bristly face with his large hands and sighed again. "What are you guys doing here, anyway?"

"Frankly, I didn't know if you were on the take," I told him, making up a story on the fly. "I'm not going out of town and leaving my parents here if they are in any danger. I wanted to check for myself that they weren't, and that this really *is* about Anthony Drake."

"I'm a cop!"

"So is your captain," I pointed out. "That hasn't stopped him from protecting Anthony Drake."

"So even though we went to school together, you didn't trust me?"

"It didn't sound like you trusted me, either," I said. "You just about flat-out accuse me of doing…something. I don't know what you thought I was hiding."

And let's face it, whatever Kyle thought? There's no way he could have been right about what I was hiding.

"I'm a detective. I don't trust anyone," Kyle said with a half grin.

"Well, I'm a—"

Charlotte!

Oh, right. He's human. He wouldn't know what a lawgiver was.

"You're a what?"

"I'm a-curious about what you found out," I said. Gunther tried not to chuckle out loud. Kyle gave me an odd look.

"I found out that for whatever reason, Anthony Drake does not want his daughter's murder solved," Kyle said. "In all the years I've been chasing this man, though, I can't even conceive of what the reason would be behind his organization calling in favors to let his daughter's murderer go free."

"Maybe he wants to be the one to take revenge?" Gunther asked.

"Maybe," Kyle said. He looked and sounded unconvinced.

"Could he have done it?" I asked him.

"I...I mean, the man is capable of some really shady stuff. I wouldn't put it past him to kill anyone if it served his agenda. But his own daughter? I have a hard time believing that."

"You didn't hear him when he came to see where Tiffany died," I shuddered. "I am so grateful that man wasn't *my* father. He was just so mean, almost blaming her for being weak enough to be killed. Ugh, it was really horrible."

"That sounds like him," Kyle said.

"And when he showed up, the dogs were so afraid of him. For a second I wondered if he did kill Tiffany, just because of how much fear all of the dogs showed. But a father killing a daughter? I just can't see it."

"Dogs can sense horrible, violent people," Aidan said. "In this part of the state, Anthony Drake is the most horrible and violent of them all."

"Yeah, maybe," I agreed. Even though I agreed, there was something about that visit, something nagging at me. Something that I felt I was missing. "Can you...um...remember that visit really well, Aidan?"

"It's a little hazy," he told me as his eyes moved briefly over to Kyle, then back. "Why?"

"I just thought that if you could remember, then..."

If you can remember, Aidan, then I can look at it through your mind with the psychic power I can't talk about in front of your quarterback boyfriend. Telepathy was only appreciated in its full awesomeness when it wasn't available to you. I felt like I was limping with half a...

Okay, I'm not gonna make jokes about limping or not having legs anymore.

"Charlotte?"

"Don't worry about it, we'll talk later."

Aidan nodded.

"Wow, you guys really *do* kind of talk in code," Kyle said. "Aidan told me that you guys were so close, it was almost like you could finish each other's sentences. I didn't realize it meant the sentences would never get finished," he laughed.

"So what now?" I asked Kyle, changing the subject.

"Well, it's almost five o'clock," Detective Roberts said, looking at his phone. "I don't know about you guys, but I'm pretty hungry. We could go grab dinner, and talk about what we each know about the case. Maybe the captain doesn't care if the case gets solved, but I do."

"Hey," Aidan broke into a mischievous smile. "I know *just* the place we should go."

"Where?" Gunther asked.

"Anthony Drake's restaurant."

CHAPTER 12

AIDAN SUGGESTED THAT GUNTHER RIDE WITH Detective Roberts. His excuse was that I would be traveling soon, and he wanted to spend as much time just the two of us as he could get. Gunther looked suspicious, but for all of Kyle's claims he trusted no one, he just nodded.

"There are some things you need to know," Aidan said as soon as the car doors slammed shut. "Micah?"

"Yeah?"

"Is Michael Hayden," Aidan said. He slowly pulled away from the curb and followed Detective Roberts SUV. "I saw the images of him in the threads of Melissa's past while she told us the story."

"Okay, that…I don't know if that makes things clearer or even muddier," I told Aidan, biting my thumbnail. "So Tiffany played a joke on a rival sorority, and it just so happens that the dog she kidnapped and winds up 'accidentally' killing is the dog of her father's right-hand man's disabled sister?"

"That does seem like an awfully convenient coincidence," my friend said. We slowed to a stop for a traffic light. "I wish I'd had my full power when Hayden stopped by your parent's shelter with Drake. Just a slight sense I got from him seems completely at odds with how his sister sees him."

"What do you mean?"

"She still sees him as caring, sweet Micah who sacrifices everything to take care of her. The snippets I got from him and that shelter? Well, serial killer vibe wouldn't be overstating it."

"I get what you mean," I agreed. "He was cold as ice, and I sensed flashes of really negative, dark emotions and thoughts, but Hayden would stuff them down and hide them almost as soon as I sensed it."

"That's pretty disciplined, I would think," Aidan observed.

"If psychopaths are disciplined, yeah, sure."

"By the way," Aidan said as the restaurant came into view. "Your boyfriend healed Melissa's phantom pains. I knew what he was doing immediately when I saw his hands moving. Sometimes this power is useful in the most random of ways." He smiled at me. "I thought you should know. I suspect Gunther is a little alarmed at some of the inequalities of our human world."

"I wish I had thought to do that," I grumbled. "I'm glad Gunther did it. He's just so much smarter than I am about magic, you know? Like, he probably could've completely healed her spinal cord so that she could walk again, but he realized that would be suspicious and unexplainable. So he did what he could. Maybe."

"Oh, he did that, too," Aidan confided. "She just won't know for a couple of years, and the doctors will likely be able to track it and explain why. It's a slower healing spell than the phantom pain one. I just wanted you to know because...I think the people getting sick and dying if they can't pay for treatment? That bothered him."

"How did you know that's what we were thinking back and forth?"

"I didn't then. I knew after it happened, though. It became the past."

"Right," I said. "Heck, I've seen it happen, and it bothers me."

"Yeah, but you know it's just the way it is. He doesn't. It was a bit of a shock to him."

"I know you haven't seen me in a while, but I have to tell you," I told Aidan as we parked in the restaurant parking lot. "I am finding myself asking why things are the way they are a lot more often than I used to."

"Goodness, Charlotte. Don't you think healing the paranormal world is enough for one person to take on?"

"Hey, if you're going to change the world? Go big or go home." I reached for the car door. "Besides, I'm not one person. I'll have a lot of help. Including you."

Aidan stared at me, his eyes narrowing gently. We watched each other for a moment as if suspended in time, hands on the car doors ready to jump out…yet neither of us moved.

Aidan's eyes grew unfocused, and as I stared into them deeply it almost looked as if they contained stars and universes that sparkled. I was so comfortable with my friend, knew him so well that his change didn't frighten me. Yet looking into his eyes, I knew that change in him was so… incredibly profound. Maybe for the first time.

"You are a thread that may weave another layer of the world, Charlotte," Aidan whispered, and I shivered at his words. "Even if you don't live up to all that you could be, if you accomplish even a tenth of what you could, the world will be so much better for it."

The whispered words hovered in the air for a moment more until the stars cleared from Aidan's eyes.

"Wow, I'm starting to sound like some freaky modern gay Gandalf," he laughed. I laughed, too, grateful for the breaking of an uncomfortable tension.

A loud knock echoed from Aidan's window as an impatient Detective Roberts urged us to get a move on.

"Let's go solve a murder," I said as I opened the door.

"While you're doing that, get the lasagna," Aidan told me. "It's fantastic."

My opinion of Kyle wasn't all that high to start. I mean, his super-suspicious detective smarmy thing wasn't all that fun to be on the receiving end of, especially in front of my parents. What had really got me, though, was how cold he had been to Aidan back at the shelter.

As the four of us walked into the restaurant, though, I did sense that Kyle was fond of Aidan. He cared about him to an extent and wasn't quite as cold as I first sensed he was.

The two, though, had precisely zero chemistry.

"A table for four?" a gentleman in meticulously pressed khaki pants asked us, reaching beneath the podium for menus.

"A booth, if you could." Kyle pointed toward the back of the restaurant. "That one in the corner with the high back? That would be perfect. We'd appreciate some privacy."

"Of course, if you will all follow me."

The restaurant was crowded even though it was early. Older couples and young families with children contributed to the loud din of the casual Italian eatery. Waiters and waitresses balancing large trays of cheesy, steaming dishes walked briskly from one end of the large room to the other.

"Here we are," the host said and stepped back. Once we all slid into the circular booth, he handed each of us a menu. I opened mine to find two pages of standard Italian choices, but no prices next to the options.

"How do you know how much it costs?" I asked the host.

"The gentleman's menu contains all the information he'll need to be able to pay for the lady's meal," he answered, smiling.

"Oh, you have *got* to be kidding me," I responded loudly.

"Charlotte, just let it go," Aidan murmured quietly.

"She's new to the place, buddy. We'll take care of her," Kyle told him. With one more quick glance of concern, the host nodded to Kyle. Once he let us know that our server would be around shortly, he headed back to the front of the restaurant.

"Okay, someone better explain to me why I basically just walked into the nineteen-fifties." I set down the sexist and exceedingly insulting menu. "No one has a problem with this? Really?"

"We're not here to protest the restaurant's misogynistic practices, Charlotte," Kyle told me quietly. "We're going to attract attention just by being here. Let's not fight two battles at the same time."

"This is absolutely offensive," I mumbled.

"Anthony Drake is really, really old-fashioned," Aidan told me.

"I don't think I understand exactly what's going on," Gunther said, confused.

"This is a ladies' menu," I told him as I waved the leather-bound book in the air. "It was so women didn't know how much money men were spending when they took them out to dinner. The assumption being, obviously, that a woman would never pay for dinner."

"To be fair, only high-end restaurants did that for the most part," Kyle said. "And it was prevalent in Europe back in the day."

"This is a casual restaurant, and this hasn't been a practice since, like, forty years ago! What kind of person is he that he still provides a ladies' menu at a casual Italian restaurant in Mickwac, Texas?"

"Someone who can do anything he wants." Michael Hayden slid into view at the front of the booth. He gazed out over the filled tables and sixty customers enjoying themselves. "If you don't like it, there are certainly other establishments to patronize. Clearly, the restaurant will not rise or fall on *your* meal."

"How would you feel if your sister was given a ladies' menu?" I asked him. "You don't think she'd be insulted?"

Michael Hayden's eyes narrowed, and I felt that emotional sheet flutter between us. He continued to be unreadable from a telepathic mental standpoint, but his expression flashed concern he couldn't conceal.

"What do you know about my sister?"

"I know she thinks you're a decent guy. Though she seemed nice, that indicates she's a pretty bad judge of character," I told him.

"I do what I need to do to protect her," he responded. "I'm sure you would do the same for your family."

"I am. That's why I'm here."

"That's not why you're here," he told me, his eyes narrowing.

"Oh? So why *am* I here?"

Hayden glared at me and then turned to Kyle.

"Detective Roberts, did your captain neglect to inform you that your investigative services were no longer needed in the Tiffany Drake case? Or do you just *like* to live on a *dangerous* edge?"

Kyle sat back and gazed calmly at Anthony Drake's assistant, but he didn't respond.

"You've given up a lot for your sister," Aidan said quietly.

"Shut up," Michael said, leaning over the table.

"I don't know you, and I don't know what *any* of you are doing here, but I suggest you order your meal and eat your meal, and then get *out*. The quicker, the better."

Pulling back, he turned and pointed a finger at Kyle.

"If you know what's good for you, Detective, you will stay away from my sister, and you will keep these nosy busybodies away from her as well. She's been through enough."

Kyle continued to stare while saying nothing.

"You folks enjoy your meal, now," Hayden finished, as he dropped his hand and walked casually away. "Terry? Comp table fourteen's meal. Anything they'd like. We have to support our local police force, now, don't we?"

"Yes, Mr. Hayden," the frightened waitress answered. Quickly, she popped up to replace him at the edge of the booth.

"Just one second, Terry," Aidan told her. She nodded and walked away nervously.

"What a tool," Kyle growled quietly.

Aidan looked around as if he wanted to say something, but couldn't quite figure out how. His gaze fell on Kyle for a few seconds. I watched his eyes narrow and his fingers dance under the table. A subtle magic whoosh blew over the table.

After just a few seconds, Kyle's face looked confused. Then he shifted slightly in the booth. A few seconds after that, he moved again. Then his face grew tense.

"Wow," Kyle said as he turned red. "Suddenly, I really have to hit the head. Gunther, you mind letting me out?"

As soon as his boyfriend's mad dash down the hall to the men's room ensured Kyle was on the other side of the door, Aidan leaned forward and whispered.

"Michael Hayden and Tiffany Drake were involved romantically. Or…no, wait. They were supposed to get married."

"How do you know that?"

"I saw it in his past."

"How did she not tell us this? And how did you *not* see this in Tiffany's past?"

"Maybe he wasn't that important to her," Aidan said. "I don't know why I see the parts that I see, not really. I can—"

"If you start giving me the whys and wherefores and codicils and addendums to your power, and why it's not perfect, save it," I whispered as Gunther broke into a grin. "Been there, done that, got the t-shirt."

~

"What are you guys talking about?" Kyle came back to the table looking much relieved of his previous pressure. Gunther slid in next to Aidan and Kyle sat across from me. "Did you figure something out?"

"Other than the fact that Michael Hayden doesn't seem to like you much? Not really," Aidan told him. "Should we order?"

"No, you should *leave*," Anthony Drake rasped as he appeared at the end of our table. "Get the hell out of my restaurant. You shouldn't be here, and you don't belong here."

I could play this one of two ways. The confrontational approach wasn't likely to get me anywhere, at least not here. I also worried about the dozens of children around the restaurant. Anthony Drake wasn't worried about getting in trouble for anything he did. I doubted beating up a girl in his restaurant would even rank very high on the concerned scale.

So, I went the other way. Even though it turned my stomach.

"Mr. Drake, we *just* want to get some dinner," I told him, as I fluttered my eyelashes and gave him my best feminine demure look. "These boys have been dragging me all over Mickwac all day, and I'm just so fatigued and hungry." I fanned myself with the abominable ladies' menu.

"Well, maybe you shouldn't be running around with these two fruits." Anthony Drake leaned over close enough that his exhalation of garlic filled my nose. "Your mother and father know that you're running around with the town perverts?"

A sparkle ash end was too good for this jerk.

What are you doing? Gunther asked.

I don't know. Talking to him. I'm going to see if I can get information about Michael and Tiffany. It'll at least make it easier for the four of us to talk, since we'll be able to explain where the information came from.

Gunther nodded imperceptibly.

"Yeah, there really aren't too many men in this town left that are *real* men, you know," I told Mr. Drake. I sat straight up and stuck my chest out as far as I could without being obscene. "I knew them when I was here before, but you're right, they are not *real men*. Not like the man that would work for you." I giggled and reached up to twirl my hair.

I felt like an offensive stereotype, and thought for sure Anthony Drake would call me on it. Yet the gangster troglodyte smiled in a friendly way, at least for a predator. He was buying it.

Kyle made a valiant attempt at keeping his facial expression unreadable, but his eyes were as wide as saucers.

"No, the men that work for me are *real men,*" Anthony Drake said proudly. "They would take care of you just the way a man should, so you don't have to do any of that pesky thinking that gets women in trouble."

"Is that what you think got Tiffany in trouble?" I asked, leaning forward to show more cleavage and fluttering my eyes like an idiot. "I'm so surprised that she didn't have someone to take care of *her.* I would've thought, you bein' the perfect Daddy and all, you would've made *sure* that she had a real man to look after her."

How on earth is this actually working?

Magic, Charlotte, Gunther said in my mind. *You're concentrating so intently on the illusion you're trying to project that you're basically hypnotizing the guy.*

I thought I can't use my ringmaster power on someone off the fairgrounds?

Not your ringmaster power, Gunther said. *This is everyday old witch magic, and you are terrifyingly effective at wrapping that dangerous man around your finger.*

I really didn't know precisely what I was doing that was making this work, so I just kept doing what I was doing.

"Of course I had my little pumpkin ball taken care of," Anthony responded with a wide smile. "I made sure she had my best man, Michael. I wouldn't have even sent her to college, but Michael insisted that we had to keep up appearances. He didn't want to wife an ignorant woman, you see."

He didn't want "to wife"? What does that even mean?

"Well, that's just wonderful," I cooed and leaned forward even further. "When did they start dating?"

"They didn't date," the gangster said, looking shocked at the suggestion. "You can't let women date. Then they think they have choices, or can change their minds. No, she was promised to Michael, and they were going to get married. That was just the way it was, you see. They didn't need to date. They had a betrothal ceremony. When she graduated from college, they'd get married. Done."

I stopped twirling my hair and stared at him,

shocked. "So, they didn't spend any time together? Or get to know each other at all?"

I could see whatever magic I had accidentally weaved around Anthony Drake was fading at my incredulous question.

Twirl, Charlotte!

What?

Twirl your hair!

I giggled again and tossed my hair, wrapping a chunk around my forefinger. As soon as I began mindlessly circling the strands, the broad smile returned to Anthony Drake's face, and he nodded.

"No, of course not! What'd it matter whether they spent any time together? Got to know each other? Tiffany was my daughter, dumb as she was. Michael's my right-hand man. He's like a son to me. Michael had to marry Tiffany if he wanted to take over."

"Why?" I asked breathlessly and fluttered my eyelashes.

"Because I said so, little girl," the gangster said proudly. "This isn't some crime family where there are rules. I make the rules. I have the money, I have the power, and I make the rules. If Michael wanted to make the rules someday, he had to marry my idiot daughter."

"Why do you keep calling Tiffany your idiot daughter?" I asked breathlessly. More eyelash fluttering. Head tilt. Hair twirl. Hold down nausea.

"Because she's a *girl*," he said. He held his hands up and looked at me like I was a moron. Which is clearly what he thought because, you know, female. "Girls are dumb. They're just stupider than men. Well, maybe not *these* men..."

"I can't do this anymore," I said. I dropped my hand and stood up in front of the dangerous crime boss. "Your beliefs belong to the dirt heap of history. How you ever got any woman to have a child with you is beyond me."

"I have my ways," he sneered, anger and treacherous threat shooting off of him as if a champagne bottle had been shaken up and then uncorked. "Believe me, no one says no to me for long. Those that do wind up dead."

"Freeze!" I snapped, my eyes narrowing.

"What are you, a cop now?"

"Darn it," I mumbled. "I really hoped it was him."

"Charlotte, what are you doing?" Detective Roberts asked as he got up.

"Sit down, fruity pants," Drake sneered.

"I think we should all just calm down," Gunther interjected. He struggled to get up.

"I think it's time for us to go," Aidan said politely but firmly. "Mr. Drake, we apologize if we caused a disruption in your restaurant. We definitely should have thought about the stress this would cause you before we showed up to eat. Your lasagna is the absolute best in the plains, though, and I would've really enjoyed it."

Anthony Drake stared at Aidan as if he didn't know what to make of him. After a few heart-pounding moments where I wasn't sure which direction this confrontation was headed, the gangster nodded and stepped back. "Appreciate the apology. Now get out."

As the restaurant watched, we headed quickly toward the door and left.

CHAPTER 13

"DOES SOMEONE WANT TO EXPLAIN TO ME WHAT the heck that was in there?" Kyle asked as soon as we were far enough away from the restaurant that no one could overhear. "Even in high school you didn't act like *that* much of a bimbo. I didn't want to cause a scene, but c'mon!"

"Have you seriously never gone undercover before, Detective Snotty?" I asked Kyle. "No pat on the back for finding out that Michael Hayden and Tiffany Drake were engaged? Well, okay, not engaged in the traditional sense, but still. No 'Atta boy, Charlotte' for finding out that Anthony Drake didn't murder his daughter?"

"How are you under the impression that you found out Anthony Drake didn't murder his daughter somehow? Did I miss something major while I was in the bathroom?" Kyle asked as he stepped up in my space. Which was annoying, especially when I couldn't teleport him back to somewhere not in my face.

"I don't think he murdered his daughter," I told Kyle defiantly. "And if you think that he did, you're a terrible detective."

"Again, know-it-all, just because you think he didn't do something? That doesn't mean he didn't do it. Believe it or not, criminals can be cagey. They lie sometimes. And you didn't even *ask* him if he killed his daughter!" the detective pointed out.

"Hey, guys…" Aidan said calmly, but Kyle ignored him.

"I didn't have to ask him if he killed his daughter. Frankly, who would ask somebody if they killed their daughter? He obviously didn't," I told him as I took a step back. "Why do you even think he did? Just because of who he is?"

As I stepped back, Kyle stepped forward.

"What's obvious to you is obvious to exactly *no one else.*"

"I, um, agree with her. Actually." Gunther said. "I don't think Drake killed Tiffany, either. Frankly, he has so little respect for women I don't think he has it in him to see her as a threat to anything he does."

"Do you even *live* in this town?" Kyle snapped at Gunther. "I know you're *her* boyfriend and all, but you don't know any of these people, do you? Why did I even bother getting civilians involved? I'm such an idiot."

"Hey, Kyle—" Aidan said as he reached for the angry detective.

"Don't touch me! This is *your* fault," Kyle told him.

Aidan dropped his hand.

"You don't have to know people to listen to them speak," Gunther said. "You don't have to have a history with people to understand them. For example, I don't think the way you're treating all of us has anything to do with us."

"Oh *really*, brainiac? Then what did it have to do with?"

"Anthony Drake insulted you in there," Gunther responded. "I can't imagine what it's like to be spoken to in that manner by such a man. Truly, I sympathize with you. Trying to serve with honor in a system designed to reward those who are corrupt...Well, it can be intolerable."

Kyle Roberts froze and stared at Gunther.

"But Charlotte didn't speak to you that way.

Neither did I. Aidan would never pass judgment on you the way that man did. We all were here for you. Charlotte was attempting to help you," Gunther said. "I *think* you know that. I do, however, suspect your frustration stems from the fact that even though you have more information, there is nothing you can do with it. In your town, these criminals are untouchable."

"Guys…" Aidan said again more insistently, but Gunther held his hand up to silence him.

"You are right, I *am* a stranger here. More of a stranger than you could possibly know, Detective Roberts," Gunther said with a smile. "The place, *this* place, is very confusing to me in many ways. What is not confusing, Detective, is that you are a good person. You mean well. You are trying to protect your people. And you are being thwarted in your sacred mission. I *understand* that produces anger. You are angry, however, at the *wrong* people."

Kyle Roberts looked down at the asphalt. Gunther's words had touched him, and the tough detective moved from angry to uncomfortable. After a few moments, he raised his head and met Gunther's eyes. "You circus people are pretty weird, you know that?"

"We have been told that, yes," Gunther returned the smile warmly.

"The dogs!" I shouted as I stared at the other three. "The dogs! At the shelter!"

"Does someone want to finish her sentence? Because I don't know what she's talking about," Kyle said to Aidan and Gunther.

"The dogs were unreasonably frightened when Anthony Drake and Michael Hayden came to see where Tiffany was killed," Gunther explained to Kyle. "I think what Charlotte is saying is that if Anthony Drake did not kill Tiffany, it must've been Michael Hayden."

"I may have been kind of a jerk a minute ago, but I'm still not convinced Anthony Drake didn't kill his daughter," Kyle pointed out. "So, it's clearly one of the two if we believe the dog fear theory."

It must be Michael Hayden, I thought to Gunther.

I agree, but how do you plan on explaining that to Kyle?

"Now that we have that all settled and before everyone breaks into a group hug, I need to let you all know that Michael Hayden is staring at us from the doorway of that restaurant. I may not have

Charlotte's...intuition, but the hair on the back of my neck is standing up," Aidan said. "I suggest we leave and have this conversation somewhere else."

It wasn't the brightest moment the four of us had, but all four of us simultaneously turned our heads to look back at the restaurant doorway. Michael Hayden was indeed staring at us without any subtle pretense. His lithe body leaned against the overhanging frame as patrons walked passed him without concern. His arms crossed, he merely watched the four of us as we watched him.

"Could he hear us?"

"He'd have to have superhuman hearing," Kyle responded without turning back.

"I want to go back and talk to Melissa," I told Detective Roberts quietly. Maybe her story would contain information that would clarify it to Kyle that Michael Hayden was the killer. "She *has* to know about her brother's relationship with Tiffany Drake. She never really got to finish her story about that. We were interrupted. By you, if you'll recall."

Let's hope something in her story will give the detective something to hang his hat on, I thought to Gunther.

"Didn't he tell us to leave his sister alone?" Gunther asked out loud.

"Does Charlotte normally do what she's told now?" Aidan asked, laughing. "That's a change in her I wouldn't have guessed."

Gunther looked sharply at Aidan and then broke into a smile. Laughing, he responded with a camaraderie I wasn't entirely sure wouldn't bite me in the butt at some later date. "No, Charlotte does not normally do what she's told. I suppose that's not a new thing, is it?"

"No. No, sir, it most certainly is not."

"Okay, how about everybody stops comparing notes on me and let's get a move on, huh?"

"They didn't even ask me for my opinion," Kyle said as he walked toward the car. "I mean, I knew you before any of them."

"Nobody wants your opinion!" I called as we all climbed into our vehicles to head back to the AOK house.

When I looked back to the doorway, Michael Hayden was gone.

The Texas sky was a bright burnt orange. After living here for many years, I knew that color meant the sun had dipped below the horizon. I felt vaguely uncomfortable at being locked out of the Magical Midway for the first time since I became ringmaster.

My old human life was something so familiar and something I had slipped into so smoothly that I didn't think spending one night out of the grounds would be that big a deal. Now that the choice to get back in time was taken from me I realized it was, and I didn't like it.

It'll be okay, Gunther said in my mind.

I didn't think I was going to feel this...adrift, I guess, I told him. *When we get back, I really want to find a way to change this. I don't like this.*

Of course, Charlotte, he told me. His eyes met mine in the rearview mirror. Even though I couldn't see his mouth, I could tell from the crinkle in his eyes he was smiling at me.

My feelings for Gunther had deepened. I couldn't imagine my life without him now.

"Here we are again," Aidan said as we pulled up. After my friend turned off the car, he quietly gazed at the houses around the circle. "Seems awfully quiet for a cul-de-sac filled with sororities. Charlotte, can you sense anything?"

I scanned each house and let my psychic fingers poke around as if I was waving a hand through water. I periodically bumped into a girl here and a girl there, but nothing stood out as suspicious. Young women studying, chatting, watching television, talking about boys. It might be a particularly conservative sorority Friday night, but nothing seemed strange or out of place.

At least it didn't until I scanned the AOK house.

"Melissa's in there by herself, and she's terrified," I gasped.

Car doors flew open and we jumped out of Aidan's car. Kyle was walking casually toward us as we began a mad dash over the ramp. We vaulted over the zigzag handrails as if we were training for the Olympics. Kyle raced after us, not understanding what prompted our mad dash toward the AOK door.

"What are you doing?" Kyle yelled at Gunther as Gunther waved his hand in front of him to slam the door open. "You can't go in there, I don't have a warrant! What the heck are you people doing? Stop!"

The three of us ignored him and raced through the door.

Anthony Drake stood in the center of the living area.

His gun was pointed at Melissa's head.

"You people need to get out," the gangster growled. "This is between her and me. My daughter's dead because of this stupid girl."

"Mr. Drake, please," I said. I slowly stepped around the room, so we were facing each other. I was the only person in the room immune to the bullets in that gun, and all I could think of was how to get myself in front of that barrel so no one else would get hurt.

"Charlotte, are you insane? Get away from him!" Kyle shouted from the door. I glanced quickly and saw he had pulled his own service revolver. "You're going to get yourself shot! Let me handle it!"

Aidan and Gunther knew I was bulletproof.

Kyle had no idea.

"Mr. Drake, Melissa is in a wheelchair," I told him. "She could not possibly have murdered your daughter."

"Hey!" Melissa said sharply, her voice shaking. "I can do anything anyone else can do!"

"I don't think this is the time, Melissa," I told her.

"Right," she said as she glanced up at Anthony Drake. "Okay, I could have. But I didn't. I didn't kill *anyone*. But I absolutely *could* have if I wanted to. Just so we're clear."

"I didn't say she killed her," he snapped at me without taking his eyes or his gun barrel from the frightened girl. "I said it was her *fault*."

The sound of young women exclaiming shock drifted in from the front porch.

Gunther, go stop them! I've got this!

Gunther nodded and ran out of the front door.

"Aidan, Charlotte, you both need to go!" Kyle commanded.

"I know you're not gonna believe me, but I can handle this," I told him. "You and Aidan need to go. Please, Kyle, just trust me."

"Are you out of your mind?" Kyle shouted. Aidan turned to his boyfriend. Rapidly wiggling his fingers, he pressed against the center of Kyle's forehead. With a whispered word no one in the room heard, Kyle's face turned placid, and his gun lowered.

"We'll be outside," Aidan said calmly. Just before he left the front hallway, he looked back at Melissa with concern. "Be careful, Charlotte."

"Yes, be *careful*, Charlotte," Anthony Drake spat at me. "I have enough bullets for both of you."

"Step back away from my sister, Tony," a voice rasped from behind me.

I knew who it was without turning around, obviously, but if he hadn't spoken, I never would've known that Michael Hayden was there. I could sense nothing from either man. They were cold, calculating sheets of glass. Robotic. No emotion, no thoughts, nothing I could read and nothing I could see.

It was why Aidan couldn't see that Michael Hayden had killed Tiffany. It was why I couldn't sense what he'd done. Maybe it was why Aidan couldn't read it in his timeline.

It was how I knew now that the chances of us all getting out of this room without someone getting shot were low.

The two men were predators. When they were ready to kill, they were dead inside.

For the first time since I had become ringmaster, I was terrified. It was as if my intuition depended upon the humanity of whoever I tried to sense, and these two men at that moment in time had *no* humanity. There was nothing for me to read. They felt nothing, they thought nothing, and so I sensed nothing. That they were human beings and yet so empty…it was horrible.

Michael Hayden had killed Tiffany. Anthony Drake would kill his sister in retaliation. And I was standing in the center of the dangerous confrontation unsure of how to protect the girl in the wheelchair.

"Your sister is the reason my daughter is dead," Anthony told him coldly.

"*You* are the reason your daughter is dead," Hayden responded just as coldly. "If you weren't such a jerk, Tony, I never would have been able to pull this off."

"It was you from the beginning?" Mr. Drake growled. "I should have known. I should have known when you screwed up Tiffany's lawyer that something wasn't right. You ungrateful—"

"Micah, I don't understand," Melissa whispered through choked tears.

"Mellie, don't be afraid," Michael said. Emotion suddenly flared from him as if someone had turned on a psychic lightbulb. "I told you I would never let anything happen to you. Nothing's going to hurt you."

"You shouldn't make promises you can't keep," the gangster sneered at his right-hand man. "Congratulations. You got me. You killed my daughter. Time to make it even, eh, *Micah*? A stupid girl for a stupid girl. That's fair, right?"

"How did you know I killed Tiffany?" Michael asked.

"When those four idiots came to the restaurant," Drake said, waving his gun in my direction, "I have the parking lot bugged. They pointed out that when we came to see where my darling Tiffany met her end, the dogs were scared. They weren't scared of me."

"To be fair, you did yell at them and kicked one of their cages, so I think they were also scared of you," I told him. I stepped closer to Melissa.

"You really don't know when to shut your mouth, do you?" the gangster responded.

"How does killing his sister solve anything?" I inched closer to the frightened girl. "Melissa didn't have anything to do with your daughter dying. Michael did it. I mean, if you're going to kill anybody, wouldn't you just kill *him*?"

"He can't kill me," Hayden said with a laugh. "He's so lazy that he has me move all of his money. He doesn't even know where half of it is."

"Don't get cocky, kid," Drake barked back. "Half of my money is still a huge pile."

Melissa's gasps echoed in the silent room as the two men stared at one another.

My hand rested lightly on Melissa's

wheelchair. As I was contemplating throwing my body across her to protect her, I had an idea.

Can I freeze two guilty people simultaneously? I asked Gunther.

What do you mean?

Michael Hayden is guilty because he killed Tiffany Drake. Anthony Drake is guilty because he's holding a gun on Melissa Hayden. I mean, they're both guilty of something, right? So can I just freeze them both?

Even if you could, how are you going to explain that to Melissa? And to both of them?

Can't I worry about that after it works and nobody gets shot?

I don't think so, Charlotte. There will be no reasonable explanation for what's taking place for any of them.

What about wiping their minds like we were going to do with Aidan?

Then all of this just happens again.

Superpowers should be much more useful in a situation like this.

"You can't kill me, Tony," Michael Hayden said quietly. "The reverse, however, is certainly not true."

My head rang as a gun went off.

CHAPTER 14

THE POLICE SHOWED UP IN FORCE, BUT I HAD TO wonder why. What was the purpose?

By the time Anthony Drake's body was removed from the AOK house, Michael Hayden had made it clear to the corrupt captain he was expecting things to run as they had before. The captain nodded as I watched him pocket a wad of bills. He didn't even try to hide it.

"I don't get it, I mean, what was it all for?" I asked Aidan as we leaned against his car. "Hayden gets away with killing Tiffany Drake and her father, the town is still under the thumb of a psychopath, the police department is still completely corrupt. Did we actually accomplish anything here at all?"

"Well, when you put it like that, it does kinda feel a little futile," Aidan said.

Michael Hayden walked across the street toward our group, and I tensed.

"I wanted to thank you for your assistance," he said as he walked up and held out his hand to shake mine. "I realize you put your life on the line to protect my sister, and that gesture did not go unnoticed by me. I wasn't anticipating the confrontation between myself and Mr. Drake quite so soon, but your actions accelerated my plan. The conclusion is satisfactory, and I wish to thank you for that."

"What happened to you?" I asked him. "Your sister *really* loves you, Mr. Hayden. She sees you as someone selfless, someone that sacrificed to protect her. But you're a cold-blooded murderer, and now you're the head of a criminal enterprise. You can't be both."

"Can't I? Yes, I imagine it's confusing for you," he smiled coldly. "It really was simply a matter of overcoming the biggest obstacle in my way."

"What obstacle was that?"

"My conscience," he said. Michael Hayden kept his hand extended for a few moments more and then dropped it. "Your parents and your animal shelter have nothing to fear from me. I wanted you to know that."

"I feel like I should thank you, but…"

"I understand. Again, I thank you for your attempt to protect Melissa. Good luck to you, Ms. Astley. I doubt we'll meet again."

The new head of our small-town Texas mob walked away from me with his head held high. The police glanced at him, but they never stared for too long. There was a new sheriff in town.

And it wasn't the sheriff.

"It's never futile fighting evil." Gunther watched the human police with fascination. "Clearly both of our worlds have a way to go, but if no one fights, the evil wins. We have to fight. Perhaps we have to fight hardest when it seems most futile."

"If I haven't told you, Charlotte, I really like your boyfriend." Aidan leaned in and bumped my shoulder with his own. "Definitely better than a pseudo-fake gay boyfriend."

"I like yours, too," I told him, bumping back.

"Well, I don't think mine is going to be mine for very long," Aidan observed with some regret, watching the handsome Kyle Roberts talking with his captain. We could hear none of what was being said, but the look on Kyle's face said it all.

"I'm a little sorry I'm going to be leaving. Frankly, I feel much closer to him after this experience. That wall that was between us? It doesn't feel like it's there anymore."

"Have you told him yet?"

"That I'm running away to the circus?" Aidan asked. I nodded, and he shook his head no. "I figured this scenario would come to a close at some point. I've been trying to figure out how to tell him. I don't want to lie to him about why am going, but it's not like I can tell Kyle the truth."

"Well, we'll be here another week, maybe two," I told him. "You have some time to figure it out. I did really want to spend some time with my parents, and we have to figure out what's going on with Tiffany Drake. I wonder if she's moved on now that her murder's been solved?"

"Is that why she was there?" Gunther asked.

"I have no idea. I don't know why ghosts do what they do."

Kyle Roberts walked across the cul-de-sac looking as depressed and forlorn as I had ever seen him. As he approached us, he nodded.

"Are you okay?" Aidan asked him. Kyle nodded again and gazed back at the house.

"I just want to get out of here," he told Aidan.

"We never did get dinner. At this point, I could eat a horse."

Gunther winced.

"Anybody feel like heading back to my parents' house? We could pick up some Costco pizzas on the way home, I think they're open for another half an hour."

"That sounds good," Kyle said. "I can let your parents know that this is all over and they shouldn't have any problems. This was never about them, or the animal shelter."

"Great, you going to follow us?" I asked him pushing myself off Aidan's car.

"I'll leave the SUV here. One of the guys can drive it back to the station. Aidan can drive me by to pick up my car later," he smiled.

"Let's do it," Aidan said as he clapped Kyle on the back.

We went to pick up real Costco pizza, and I wondered if it would taste different than the magical slices that Jeannie manifested for me at the Magical Midway.

Ain't nothing like the real thing, baby.

The four of us sat on the back porch of my

parents' house drinking iced tea and slurping down the ultimate cheesy pizza slices on the planet. Lights flickered from the Magical Midway, and I felt a pang of loneliness being cut off for another eight hours.

"I just don't want to talk about it," Kyle said in response to Gunther's question about Michael Hayden and the new crime organization in town. "I'm so tired of going in circles and never getting anywhere. This wasn't why I became a cop."

"I get it," Gunther said.

"Hey, does someone want to show me the circus?" Kyle asked. "I never actually got to see it when we were here before. I was at the immediate crime scene almost exclusively. I've never gotten to walk around a circus when it's closed. It just seems kind of cool."

"I…um, I…"

"I can take you," Aidan said. He pushed his chair out. "Charlotte did come to visit with her parents, and she's barely seen them since you got here because of all this. Besides, we have some things to talk about."

"Are you dumping me?" Kyle asked as he stood up. "Because, frankly, if you're dumping me, I'd rather not have that done while walking around a circus. You would totally ruin the cool factor if you dumped me while I was getting to do something that not a lot of people get to do."

"Just come on," Aidan laughed. "So suspicious!"

"Aspect of the job, bean counter."

The two laughed affectionately and walked down the back stairs and out into the dark night.

"Heck of a day," Gunther said. He moved his chair closer so he could take my hand. "Are you okay? I know that you weren't in any danger, but I can't believe that experience was easy."

"No, it wasn't, but yeah, I'm okay."

"Good. It was frustrating for me. I want to help."

"You *did* help. It helped just knowing you were there. That I could count on you to keep those other people out of the house and safe."

"That's good, I'm glad," he said, and he squeezed my hand.

We sat quietly and listened to the sounds of owls hooting and cicadas humming. A warm breeze rustled the cedar trees beneath the clear sky.

"I love you," I whispered to Gunther without turning to face him. I felt his hand gently brush my hair back from my face. "I just wanted you to know."

"Why was that so hard for you?" he asked me quietly.

"I don't know."

The wind continued to rustle the leaves. The owls hooted. The silence was full and heavy.

"Thank you," he said after a few minutes.

"For what? For telling you?"

"That, yes," he said and moved his chair even closer and put his arm around me. "Mostly for loving me. That's a sacred thing, Charlotte. I don't take it lightly." Gunther leaned in, and I could feel the energy in the air.

"Don't," I told him, pulling back. "Remember what happened the last time you tried to kiss me. I don't want you to get hurt."

"I'll chance it," he chuckled, still leaning in.

"I made you bleed last time!"

"Charlotte," he whispered as he placed his hands on either side of my face and gently turned me to him, "it'll be fine. I promise."

I closed my eyes and held still. he leaned in. I felt a feathery touch on my lips, and light pressure. It was the most gentle and most chaste of kisses, but my stomach fluttered and jumped.

"You see?" He pulled back. "One kiss, no bruises, and no blood. I'm fine, so are you."

"Ummm hmm," I mumbled, shivers still

running down my spine. My head was a little dizzy. I could see stars exploding in the darkness behind my eyelids.

"Charlotte?"

"Ummm hmm?" I said.

You can open your eyes now, he said in my head.

I opened them, and as my eyes cleared, Gunther's face came into focus. His expression was gentle and loving. A little amused. I wanted nothing more than to jump into his arms and kiss him. It was like an ache.

Maybe someday, he thought.

"You promised you wouldn't read my mind," I whispered to him.

"I promised no such thing. In fact, I promised you that I probably would read your mind because I was so new to telepathic communication," he pointed out.

"You're not new anymore."

"No, I guess I'm not. But I'm still not going to promise you that."

"Charlotte! Come quick!"

Gunther was instantly alert. "Was that Aidan?"

"I think so!"

"Charlotte!" Aidan's voice screeched louder. "Something's happened to Kyle, you have to come quick!"

"Oh my gosh, what now?" I asked Gunther. We jumped up from the table and ran down the stairs.

"Explain to me what the hell is happening to me!" Kyle shouted. He stomped his hooves and bucked.

Oh my.

"Charlotte will be able to, Kyle, but you have to calm down!"

I ran toward Aidan and the four-legged Kyle only to smash headfirst into an invisible wall that felt as solid as concrete. A great clang echoed from the collision, and I landed with force on my rear end.

"What was that? What was that? What is happening? Why do I have hooves? Am I on drugs?" Kyle reared up in a panic. "I've lost my mind, haven't I? All the years on the police force have finally broken my sanity in two. That has to be it."

As the newly shifted centaur paced nervously just within the borders of the Magical Midway, Aidan stood beside him looking baffled.

"I'm going to go get Ningul," Gunther told me and ran toward Aidan. "Can you keep him calm?"

Aidan nodded. Gunther raced deeper into the fairgrounds.

"I look like a horse. I look like a freakin' horse!"

"You don't look like a *horse*, exactly," Aidan walked forward with his hands up. "I mean, yes, the bottom part of you is horse-like, but from the waist up you're still the same guy you always were."

"What is this? What am I? What did you do to me?"

"You're a centaur, brother," Ningul said as he galloped up with Fiona on his back. "This midway shows people who they really are, who they could be if they choose."

"Oh my God. You're a horse," Kyle whispered.

"I'm not, and neither is he," Fiona said as she slid down off her boyfriend's back. "Calm yourself down there, copper. It could have been worse. You could have been a leprechaun."

"I heard that!" one leprechaun shouted from within a nearby yurt.

"I must be insane. I'm losing my mind," Kyle said over and over to himself as members of the Magical Midway moved by ones and twos toward the drama. "You're all...It's like you walked out of a storybook...What are you people?"

"We're paranormals, Kyle," I told him as I stood up and brushed the dust off my derrière. "We're all paranormals, and so are you."

Samson just asked if he can take down the illusion, Gunther asked.

Yep.

Good. I'll tell him.

In the blink of an eye, the Magical Midway return to normal. A cheer went up across the fairground.

"Oh my God, how many of you are there?" Kyle choked after the cheer. Gunther came racing back to the clearing.

"Kyle," Aidan said as he walked closer. He held out his hand to his boyfriend and simply stood two feet from him, waiting. "I promise you that everything will be okay. Just take my hand and relax. We'll explain everything to you, and it will all be okay."

Kyle stepped back and forth, side to side the way any nervous horse would in a situation where they were unsure. After a few moments, Kyle's chest heaved with a great deep breath, and he walked forward slowly to grab Aidan's hand.

"Good, that's good," Aidan told him. "Now, relax and simply decide you want to be in your human form again. Take a deep breath, close your eyes, and see yourself as you've always known yourself to be."

Kyle shimmered and returned to his human form.

Those watching clapped.

"Guys, come on, go back to your tents and yurts," I told them. "He's a friend, let us help him through this. He doesn't need an audience."

"Yeah, but we want to watch," Rhodia, a slightly obnoxious werewolf, complained.

"Guys, have some respect."

"We would if you were on *this* side of the boundary," Rhodia smarted off.

"I'll be back tomorrow morning. You *really* want to be the first thing I have to deal with when I come back? After the days I've had?"

"Our ringmaster jumped in front of a bullet to save a human!" Grog, the head of the goblin family, bragged.

"I heard she killed a gangster with her bare hands! Tore 'im to pieces, she did," Luca of the satyrs said proudly.

"None of that happened, and I think we're getting really off-topic here." I crossed my arms. "Guys, let us help Kyle. Go. Shoo."

"Well, that was rude," Grog mumbled. He and the others turned to walk away.

Kyle looked around at the assorted creatures, back to me, back to Aidan. Then he turned and stared at Ningul still in centaur form. The confident detective raised his hand toward the centaur, pointed a finger up in the air and then…

His eyes rolled back in his head as he collapsed, unconscious, to the ground.

"*This* is one of your human lawgivers?" Fiona asked with a raised eyebrow. "Not very tough if you ask *me*."

"I *didn't* ask you," I told her.

CHAPTER 15

"So I'm a centaur?" Kyle asked as we sat across from each other on the ground.

"Yes," I told him again for the tenth time. "Again, I understand that this is very difficult for you to comprehend. You're going to have to make a decision, though, about whether you want to be a paranormal or whether you want me to make it so you just go back to being human. You know, the way you were before."

"It's entirely up to you, Kyle," Aidan told him for the ninth time. Or maybe it was ten times. Or perhaps we had all been sitting out here on our rumps in the dirt at the Magical Midway border for days and days and days, and we were never

ever going to get to the end of this
conversation…

Okay, that's just what it *felt* like.

"It is challenging for our kind to function in
the human world, Kyle," Ningul told him again. "I
would strongly recommend to you, as the leader
of the centaurs at the Magical Midway, that you
join us. At least join us for a time."

"You want to figure out what you are before
you give it up, don't you?" Fiona asked him.

"None of this makes any sense to me," Kyle
told Fiona.

"Yeah, Charlotte had that deer in the path of a
hungry lion look to her when she first became
ringmaster, too," Fiona told him as she patted him
on the shoulder.

"I did not."

"You kind of did."

"Anyway, I can't do anything until tomorrow,
Kyle, so you have all night to think about it. Talk
to Aidan. He pretty much just went through this a
few hours ago, so he might be better to chat with
than me."

"How did you make your decision?" Kyle
asked him.

"My situation was a little bit different," Aidan
told him and shifted on the ground. "I have a

pretty important role to play in the paranormal world. If I decided not to stay, it's possible some pretty bad things would've happened. It wasn't a hard decision for me because it wasn't really about what I wanted."

"If it had only been about what you wanted, would you have stayed a paranormal? Or would you have changed back?"

"I would've stayed a paranormal, even if I wasn't important," Aidan told him with a wide smile. "There's so much magic in the world. It's amazing to me how much was there that I just never saw. I might go back to the human world someday, but if I do it will be with a much greater appreciation of how precious and sacred the world is."

"Should I go get the boys with the drum circle? Are we going to all start praying now?" Fiona asked sarcastically. "You all have super pretty words and all, but you're making this all sounds way more romantic than it really is. We are basically in the middle of a paranormal war, here. This isn't all unicorns and sparkles."

"If you came from the human world and all of this was mythological to you, Fiona, you would understand what Aidan is saying," Gunther said.

"Oh, I totally understand what Aidan is

saying. What I'm saying is no one should romanticize the decision that boy is about to make," Fiona disagreed. She stood up and looked down upon the group seated in a semicircle on the earth. "We are in a precarious situation. Picking up new paranormals that don't know the first thing about any of this stuff...Frankly, it's a complication."

"Fiona, you are my heart and my soul, and I understand what you're saying," Ningul told her gently. "But he is of my blood. He is Centaur. It is his choice and his choice alone. It is not about our convenience. We will do what we must to protect him. Whatever he chooses. It is my duty to do so."

Fiona's eyes shined with unshed tears. She nodded.

"Hey, now, I realize that I'm a little blown away by all the things that are happening here, but I don't need anyone to protect me," Kyle told Ningul defensively. "In the human world, I'm a cop. I'm a damn good one. If I decide to stay and be a horse man no one's going to need to take care of me, thanks."

"If you decide to stay and be a *horse man*?" Fiona asked.

"Yes?"

"Don't *ever* say *horse man* again," Fiona told him crossing her arms.

Kyle swallowed and stared at the fearsome Fiona.

"Understood," he said quietly.

My mother ran down the pathway toward the back of the property where the Magical Midway sat.

"Mom? It's two o'clock in the morning, what on earth are you doing up?"

Her bare feet were dusty as she pulled an old terrycloth robe around her more tightly and nodded to the assembled group. "That hideous man is in my bedroom," my mother told me. "He's looking for his daughter, and I can't explain to him…Well, frankly, I'm explaining it to him just fine. He's just *not* listening. Do you have any ringmaster powers that can banish a ghost? At least from my bedroom? It's been a long day."

"Argh! I cannot juggle one more thing right now!" I complained. My mother raised her eyebrow at me. "I'm sorry, Mom. I'm just tired, too. Can't you just make him happy with your power and make him go away?"

"No one could make *that* man happy, Charlotte," my mother responded. "I've tried. Believe me, I've tried."

"Well, you know what they say," Kyle said with a laugh. We all looked at him.

"Everyone is supposed to go for the juggler!"

We all stared at the overtired police officer with the punny repertoire.

"Oh, come on. No one's heard that joke? It's a circus joke! No?"

Silence.

"Are you *sure* you don't want me to wipe your memory?" I asked him.

As we trudged up the path and into the house, no one raced. Everyone was tired and emotionally drained from the events of the last few days. I also suspected that absolutely no one wanted to talk to or help Anthony Drake's ghost. His daughter had been bad enough, but him? The man was such a horrible human being in life. I doubted that death improved on him.

"This is *your fault*," the gruff, sparkling man hissed at me as I walked into my parents' bedroom. My father was sitting up in bed with his head leaning on his hand.

"I tried to explain, but—"

"I don't need lessons on life and death from the dogcatcher," Drake bellowed while pointing at my father. Dad shrugged and held up his hands in defeat. "This is *your* fault, and you're going to fix it."

"Dude, there is very little that happened in your life or the lives of those people around you that wasn't *directly* your responsibility or your fault." I flopped down on a chair at the foot of my mother's bed. "There is no *fixing* dead. Get out of my parents' bedroom. Go explore. I mean, you haunted people throughout your life. Why don't you give it a rest? Try something new for a change?"

Aidan tried to muffle a laugh.

"How *dare* you talk to me that way?" Mr. Drake raged. "Do you have any idea who I am? What I'm capable of?"

"Oooh, scary ghost. So loud. Eeek. Someone help me," I deadpanned, rolling my eyes. "You're a ghost! You're dead. You have no power over the living. None. Nada. Zip. Zilch. Ze—"

"I get it," he cut me off. For the first time since I had the unfortunate displeasure of meeting

Anthony Drake, I saw a flash of fear pass behind his sparkling eyes. "No need to rub it in."

"Go out of the house, follow the path, find a big house that looks like it's all broken down and scary, but it's really not. That's the haunted house," I told him, pointing. "Your daughter's probably in there making everyone's life miserable. Well, everyone's *death* miserable."

"What have you done to my daughter?" he barked at me again.

I sighed.

"Go. Follow the path, find the haunted house, talk to her yourself. She's a ghost, you're a ghost. I'm sure you guys have lots to talk about with regards to what you're going to do with the rest of your eternity," I told him.

The specter of Anthony Drake blurred as he flew out the door.

"Well, that wasn't very nice, Charlotte, but thank you for getting him out of my bedroom," my mother said. "Your father and I tried talking to him, but that man just doesn't want to listen to anyone."

"Welp, he's got an eternity to learn, doesn't he?"

We hugged goodnight, and my parents' bedroom emptied out of all the middle of the night visitors. As Aidan, Kyle, Gunther, Fiona, Ningul and I made our way back down the path, I heard a squeak.

"What was that?" Kyle asked.

"Opossum?"

"That was a bat," Gunther said and stopped walking. "That's not good."

"There's a lot of bats in central Texas," I told him, confused at his concerned reaction. "They don't really bother you unless they're sick. It sounded like it came from up there." I pointed to the tree along the path.

"I'm not sick," a squeaky little voice responded.

"That's *really* not good," Gunther said again.

"Who's there?" I called.

"Just me," the squeaky voice responded. It was followed by the sound of leathery flapping. I felt a rush of wind along my cheek. "Name's Cama. Don't worry. I'm not here for you. Or you. Or you," I felt a slight pressure on the top of my head, and the rush of wind disappeared. "The reader knows why am here. I'm not here for any of you. I'm here for the new ones."

"Is there a *bat* sitting on my *head*?" I asked Gunther, who stared just a bit above my face. He nodded yes.

"Is the bat talking?"

He nodded yes.

"Wow. That's really cool," Kyle marveled. He also stared at the top of my head. "That's a *huge* bat."

"How big?"

No one answered me.

"*How* big?"

"Wait," Cama chirped. I felt gentle scurrying at the top of my skull. "That's better. Not as big, and it makes the hair a little softer because I'm not as heavy."

"Someone please tell me how big this thing is…"

"I don't have to be big, so now I'm not big. I was just having a hard time wrapping my feet around that branch. That's a thick branch."

"Why are you sitting on my head?"

"Because you have the softest hair," Cama squeaked. "And it smells the best. Don't worry, though, I won't take any strands. I'm not here for that."

"Why would I care if you took a strand of my hair?"

"Because if Cama takes a strand of your hair, Charlotte, it could portend your death," Gunther told me quietly.

"That's ridiculous."

"I'm a *horse*, and you think a murderous bat is ridiculous?" Kyle asked me.

"First of all, you're *not* a horse, handsome," Cama squeaked and then clicked at Kyle as if chastising him. "Second, I don't kill anybody. I just…pull threads. Of hair sometimes. And, okay, often people die terrible deaths after I do it. But I don't *kill* anybody."

"Often?" Gunther asked.

"I think he means always," Aidan told him.

"Often, always, same thing," Cama said. "And I am a *lady* bat, thank you very much."

"While all this is fascinating, I have a *bat* on my *head*," I pointed out as I looked to each person most emphatically not moving to help me *get the bat off my head*.

"I think she wants you to *congratulate* her," Cama told the men surrounding me. "It's a great honor to have a bat nest in your hair. You people are treating it like it's no big deal. It's a huge deal."

Suddenly, Aidan jumped and smiled at the top of my head.

"Charlotte, Cama can help you cross," he said.

"Help me cross what?"

"The boundary into the Magical Midway," he said and his eyes unfocused just slightly. "Cama is a paranormal bat, and her powers in the night are very strong. Bats have the power to find ways around almost any boundary, and because of what they do they can take someone with them. I think she can get you into the Magical Midway."

"Well, of course I can," Cama clicked and chittered.

"How?"

"Why do you care?" Cama asked. I heard the leathery flap of tiny wings and felt movement on top of my head. "I just *can*. I need to go in. Do you want to go in with me? If you do, let's walk. Walk, walk, walk. You people talk *too much*. Let's go."

"Go where?"

"To the haunted house? What have we been talking about?"

I…just walked. After dealing with Samson for months, I'd learned when to ask questions and when to just give up understanding and do what I'm told.

CHAPTER 16

THE SOUND OF TIFFANY DRAKE AND ANTHONY Drake arguing was loud, obnoxious, and it made my teeth ache from the pounding vibrations. Finding them in the haunted house was easy. You just had to follow the shouting.

No other ghosts were in the room with them. Everyone must've given up on consoling the new arrivals and hid.

"Well, I see that I was sent to the right place," Cama muttered. She flew from the top of my head and circled around the two ghosts.

"Ahhhhhhhhh! A bat! It's a bat!" Tiffany screeched, swinging her sparkly, translucent arms at Cama. Her hands and elbows passed through

the little animal's body repeatedly, but Tiffany
kept striking out.

The bat flew in a circle around the two and
then slowly picked up speed. Cama flew faster,
and then faster, and then quicker still as black
lines of dark light appeared as if the bat was
wrapping the two ghosts in a cocoon made of
shadows. The more circled lines appeared, the
more muffled their shouting and screams.

"There," Cama said. She flew back to admire
her handiwork. Hovering in the air, she clicked
and squeaked a few times. "Time to call Mom."

"Step back," Gunther said urgently. His hand
flew across my body and pushed me toward the
wall. "As far as you all can against the wall. Do it,
now!"

"Why?" Kyle asked as Aidan grabbed him and
pushed him back. In the corner across the room,
Ningul had placed his body in front of a pale
Fiona.

"Should we leave?" I asked him, worried.

"It's too late," Gunther whispered and nodded
toward the center of the room.

A dark swirl of shadows seemed to spin into
being out of nothing in front of Cama. In three
blinks of an eye, the shadows elongated and grew

tall. Finally, they coalesced into the shape of a woman.

The two ghosts stared in horror at a face I couldn't see.

Arms moved animatedly, but we heard nothing.

Tiffany and Anthony pointed to each other, their mouths moving and fists raising. Despite watching what looked like a lively conversation I could hear only silence.

The silence was like a thing, so thick and so heavy I was afraid to speak, so dense that it seemed like its own sound. The shadows swallowed everything other than the flapping of Cama's tiny, leathery wings.

What is that? I thought to Gunther.

Death, he thought back, and I could hear the awe and fear in his mind's voice. *One form, in any case. A form of it reserved for those that die with no repentance for the evil they have done. I didn't even think it was real. I thought it was just a story used to scare children.*

The shadows swirling around Tiffany and Anthony moved faster and faster, spreading over them and filling in the gaps between the lines. They shook their heads no, apparently begging for some reprieve that the silent shadow woman decided not to give them.

The inky darkness circling them suddenly swallowed them both whole. It then contracted and disappeared. Only the shadow woman and the bat remained.

Why couldn't we hear what they were saying? I asked Gunther.

I don't know. I think it's because we're not dead.

The shadow woman continued to stare at the spot that Tiffany and Anthony had disappeared from. The sound slowly returned to the room. While I could still hear Cama's wings flap, I could also hear the cicadas from outside the haunted house, the creaking of the wood. Despite sound and feeling returning to normal, the shadow woman remained.

"The six of you are pure of heart," a raspy voice echoed from within and around the shadow woman. "As long as it remains so, you have nothing to fear from me."

With a roar, the darkness dissolved and disappeared.

"Oh, I am *totally* going with you guys," Kyle said with wonder. "Talking bats? Shadows of death? Divine punishment? This is like the *best* Dungeons & Dragons game *ever*."

I stared at Kyle Roberts and marveled at his little boy excitement. With a sigh, I buried my face in Gunther's shoulder and took comfort as his arms wrapped around me.

"Oh, come on, you guys didn't find that just a *little* bit cool?" Kyle asked.

"Ya, that will wear off, ya kin?" Fiona told him. She leaned against the wall trying to catch her breath. "Just hope that wears off before yer a ghost yerself."

"I'm glad you're going with us," Aidan told Kyle.

"Yeah, me, too." Kyle smiled.

"Me, too," Cama chirped. "We are going to have such fun!"

"Wait, what do you mean?" I reluctantly pulled my head from Gunther's muscular chest and looked at the bat. "*You're* going with us?"

"Yeah. I like you guys." Cama flapped excitedly.

"You can't," I told her. I wracked my brain for any excuse I could think of as to why the prelude to eternal doom couldn't just hitch a ride with us. "I mean, I have a cat. So does Gunther. Not for nothing, but my folks are nervous enough as it is. A death bat at the Magical Midway? They're never going to come out of their yurts. Come on, you don't really want to go with us, do you?"

"I *do* want to go with you, and my mom *said* I could go with you," Cama singsonged as she flew around the room. Pausing to hover, her inky eyes stared at me. "Should I get my mom so you can talk to her?"

The six of us shouted no with such incredible pitch and precision it practically sounded like a chorus.

"Good, that's settled, then," Cama pronounced. She flew up and settled down in my hair.

A bat. Samson glared at Cama. The little bat was flying around the great room of the yurt, knocking things over. *You decided to adopt a bat.*

"I didn't, like, *decide* to adopt a bat, Samson," I told the cat as we sat on the bed. "I told you, Cama showed up because of Anthony and Tiffany Drake, and she just decided that she wanted to stay."

A flying rodent, Samson observed coldly.

"Bats are not rodents," I corrected. "They are not even remotely related to rodents."

Let's find out if they taste different, the cat said. He stood up and bared his teeth and tensed to pounce on Cama.

"No! Bad cat! You are not going to eat the bat!" I told Samson as I shook my finger at him. The black cat slowly turned his head. If he had eyebrows, I was sure he would be raising only one.

What did you just call me?

"Samson, come on. There's nothing we can do about it, and since it happened on the Magical Midway, and you probably know more about that bat and that shadow woman than I do, you probably also know that. So quit giving me guff," I told him.

First, the stupid kitten. Now the silly bat. It's like I'm living in a circus, Samson grumbled and made his way over to his favorite bookcase and pillow.

"You *are* living in a circus," I called after him.

I'm not talking to you right now.

Ethel Elkins' door opened, and she walked out. Devana followed a respectful distance after her and smiled.

"We almost have the whole coven," she murmured as she scanned the crowd.

"What are you talking about?" I asked her.

"Three from the human world, three from the

paranormal world." She waved her hand in our direction.

I looked at Gunther in confusion. And then I realized.

Kyle, Aidan, and I were from the human world.

Ningul, Fiona, and Gunther were from the paranormal world.

"The balance, Charlotte," Devana said with a smile. "I told you that the world seeks balance. The universe is bringing it together here."

"Or not," Cama tittered and did a loop the loop in the center of the room.

"*Why is that death bat here?*" Ethel Elkins snapped, her eyes narrowing.

"Because Mom decided *you* needed some balance, old woman." Cama flew by her face. "You know Mom hates when things are decided. Everyone gets a chance. You're making it sound like nobody does. No more of that."

Ethel Elkins' fists balled and her shoulders tensed. The old lady's mouth worked open and shut like an angry fish again. Pulling her muumuu straight, she leaned forward and stuck a finger out toward the flying bat.

"Your mother is—"

"Yeeeeeeeeeeeees?" Cama flew straight up to

Ms. Elkins' face and hovered. The bat's inky eyes looked amused.

Ethel stared for a moment, gritting her teeth.

"Wise," she hissed through clenched teeth.

"I'll tell her you said so!" the bat said. She flew backward and zigged. "I won't tell her what you were gonna say! She'll like the wise better. Yep, very much so."

"Everyone fancies himself a weaver of fate today," Ethel mumbled.

"No fate! No fate, no prophecy, no for sure! It's also severe, and also not very serious. That's why it's *so much fun!*"

"I. Hate. Bats," Ms. Elkins groused.

"Oooh, hate isn't perfect," Cama cooed and danced around the great room. "You shouldn't do that. Hate is bad. Just ask Anthony and Tiffany Drake!"

"Who are Anthony and Tiffany Drake?" Devana asked.

"Nobodies. A waste of time," Ethel Elkins told her.

"No one's *ever* a waste of time!" Cama called. "And you wonder why mama wants me to come here! Silly old woman!"

Ethel Elkins turned around and stomped back into her room. Devana moved to follow her, but the old woman slammed the door in her face. The huntress sighed quietly and turned back to the room with a sad smile.

"I really want to understand what happened here," I told the room. "But I'm tired. I'm tired, it's three o'clock in the morning, and I just don't have the energy to parse through whatever drama this is. Let's all get some sleep. It will all be here tomorrow."

"Not *me*, I'm going to go explore." Cama raced toward the door. Aidan opened it for her, and out she went.

"Um, we don't have enough bedrooms in here," Gunther pointed out. "There another yurt?"

"Ningul and I are going to head back to his house. Charlotte can add Kyle's house tomorrow in the centaur village after she's got some sleep," Fiona grabbed Ningul's hand. She was almost to the door before she turned and smiled. "Welcome to the family, Kyle. And Aidan. It's good to have you here."

They smiled warmly back at her, and then she and Ningul left.

"The centaur village?" Kyle asked.

"Tomorrow," I told him. "I'm tired. You and Aidan go bunk in Gunther's room. There are a few places to sleep. Gunther and I can sleep in my room."

"Let me grab my kitten," Gunther said as he walked briskly toward his door. I could feel an excitement flowing off of him, and it was making me blush.

Moments later he exited his room carrying a sleepy kitten wrapped in what looked like pajamas. The guys all murmured good night.

"I don't know *what* you're so excited about," I told him as we walked toward my door. "Remember, we can't even kiss without severe bodily injury, so whatever's making you super happy right now? It ain't gonna happen. Like, ever."

"Do you want to know what's making me happy, Charlotte? It's that I get to be near you," he said softly. He walked across my room and transferred Delilah to an overstuffed chair in the corner. Samson hopped up on the same chair Delilah slept in and curled himself protectively around Gunther's kitten. The two began to softly purr.

"That's so sweet," I whispered.

"Don't say it too loud, they'll realize they're

cute and start fighting," Gunther whispered back. We both chuckled.

Each of us took turns brushing our teeth and changing behind the privacy panel into our pajamas. I was in a t-shirt and sweatpants. He emerged wearing blue proper PJs with teddy bears on them. I giggled.

"My mom," he said as he spun around to show off his sleepwear. "She loved teddy bears, and she always used to put a different one in bed with me each night. I guess it makes me feel…I don't know, not so alone. And it seems vaguely better for a grown man to wear these than to actually sleep *with* a teddy bear."

"I think you look very handsome in them," I told him. He smiled and grabbed the pillows and an extra blanket from my closet to sleep in the sitting area.

But I didn't want him to.

"I…"

"Yes, Charlotte?" Gunther asked as he turned.

"Um…never mind," I told him as I waved off the invitation I would extend. The frustration I felt was immense, but I couldn't risk it. Not that I thought anything improper could or would happen. Even just sleeping next to me was like sleeping next to a metal robot. I could have a nightmare and crack his skull open.

"No, what?" he asked as he continued to make the bed.

"It's nothing. I just thought since, like, we couldn't really *do* anything anyway it wouldn't really be improper or anything if you slept in the bed," I told Gunther as I stared at the blue comforter.

Silence.

"It's just, I know the couch is uncomfortable, and the bed is so huge, and it just seems silly, but then I remembered that I have, like, armor and I could really hurt you and…Well, I'm kind of a violent sleeper, and so I decided—"

While I had been prattling on like a complete moron, Gunther had come up behind me. His hands lightly resting on my shoulders brought my nervous babbling to an instant halt. I could feel his breath on the back of my neck, and it made me shiver.

"Charlotte," he whispered. "If we didn't live in a circus, sleeping in the same bed would be a major decision. It would be a decision we undertook after talking about the ramifications, talking about what we wanted out of our relationship, where it was going. I would like nothing more than to fall asleep with you in my arms. But you're tired, and you've only just told me that you love me."

"I do love you," I whispered staring down at the empty bed.

"I believe you, and I love you, too. More than you know," he said with a charming little laugh. "And because I love you, I'm going to sleep on the couch. Not because I want to, mind you. Because I think it's the right thing to do."

Now I felt like a hussy. Because after his little speech I really, *really* wanted to sleep in the bed with him. Like, *so* much.

But I knew he was right.

We had experienced a lot of emotion, and a lot of bonding. We hadn't done a lot of talking about our relationship and where it was going. A step like this…it didn't seem like a big step for some people, I'm sure. For the two of us?

I knew it was. It mattered. It might even be the only intimate bonding we would ever be able to have. And I loved Gunther for taking it so seriously.

"Oh, Charlotte," he laughed as he turned me around and hugged me affectionately. "I do love you. I can practically hear your brain sputtering in all different directions. Here, let me tuck you in. *That* I think we can do."

He pulled back the comforter and gently placed his hand behind my elbow to guide me into bed. I laid my head back on the pillow, and he pulled my covers around me. Brushing my hair from my face, Gunther leaned over and kissed me on the forehead.

"I love you, ringmaster," he said as he smiled. "We'll figure it all out. I promise."

I sighed as he shut off the light.

Tomorrow would no doubt bring more confusion, more prophecies, maybe another death bat or two. For tonight, though, I felt loved and cared for and like everything would be okay. With Aidan joining the circus, that feeling had only grown.

Enjoy that while it lasts, Samson said from the corner.

I did.

Go grab *Irrelephant Omens*, the next book in the Magical Midway series right now!

FIND A TYPO? LET US KNOW!

Typos happen. It's sad, but true.

Though we go over the manuscript multiple times, have editors, have beta readers, and advance readers it's inevitable that determined typos and mistakes sometimes find their way into a published book.

Did you find one? If you did, think about reporting it on leanneleeds.com so we can get it corrected.

www.ingramcontent.com/pod-product-compliance
Lightning Source LLC
Chambersburg PA
CBHW031604240626
47153CB00002B/634